Jim River Boy

MJ Ulmer

This novel is a work of fiction. The James River and the "Stone Church" mentioned herein do exist; however, the events held there, as described in this book, as well as all other names, characters, incidents, places and dialogues, are products of the author's imagination and are not to be construed as real. Any resemblance to actual events or persons, living or dead, is coincidental.

Scripture quotations are from:
New Revised Standard Version (NRSV) © 1989 National Council of the Churches of Christ in the United States of America. Used by permission. All rights reserved worldwide.

Copyright © 2022 by Jeanette Ulmer (MJ Ulmer)

Cover image by Jeanette Ulmer (MJ Ulmer) © 2022

International Standard Book Number (ISBN):
979-8-9859-605-0-1 (paperback)
979-8-9859-605-1-8 (ebook)

First edition. 2022

Printed in the United States of America

All rights reserved. No unlawful scanning, uploading or electronic sharing of any part of this book without permission from the author / publisher. If you would like to use material from the book, prior written permission must be obtained. Contact the author at MJUlmer.com.

Library of Congress Cataloging-in-Publication Data

ACKNOWLEDGEMENTS

Glory to God, through whom all things are possible! I am honored to use my talents to further His kingdom.

Several of my friends and family blessed me with their time and knowledge, prayerfully reading drafts of this book and providing feedback based on their varied perspectives. Much heartfelt appreciation goes to Harlan, Hilary, Bobbi Jo and Tracey. To Andrea for editing. To Tonya for design insight and feedback. Thank you all for stepping forward. I am blessed to have you in my life!

To the handful of people who knew about my vision and ambitions for this book; who asked how my writing was going and encouraged me along the way - you know who you are. And God knows. Thank you for believing in me. I am truly grateful.

To my parents, siblings, nieces and nephews, B.H. and A.H. You mean the world to me. I hope I make you proud.

For those who search for healing
Forgiveness is a promise
Love is a choice

CHAPTER 1

The James River, South Dakota – July 2005

Thub-dub.... Her heartbeat throbbed inside her ears, resonating beneath the water... *Thub-dub... How much can a heart slow down before it's too slow to support a life? Thub-dub... So this is what death is like? Your heart just slows down so much it stops completely? Thub-dub... It doesn't hurt as much as I imagined.*

She'd once read that a person could go five minutes without air, five days without water and five weeks without food. *Or was that three minutes, three days and three weeks?* Her anxiety rose as quickly as the water and through her muddled thoughts she couldn't remember exactly what the stats were. She did know she couldn't hold her breath for three minutes, let alone five.

The murky James River water had quickly poured into the car from the shattered driver's side window, as the frame sunk into the just-enough-to-cover-a-vehicle depth. Its shallows allowed the sun to heat its water to a lukewarm temperature and in the heat of mid-July the river was balmy and thick. Claire's first instinct was to unfasten her seat belt and escape. That's what a normal, sane person would do. They would save themselves if possible. She unclicked, but instead of swimming free from this would-be grave, she sat there while water swirled around her, floating her to the roof of the car and inching up her torso until it loomed just below her chin like a vat of witch's brew. The seconds quickly ticked by.

Of what use was it anyhow? This life of hers. She had failed her family, her child, herself and most miserably she had failed God to the point that atonement, she felt, was impossible. Suicide had been planned out in her mind multiple times these past few years so she was prepared to simply float in the dingy water until death found her. If it wasn't going to be this slow moving river it would be her shed-turned-garage with a tightly closed door and exhaust fumes to usher her on.

She felt calm, relieved even, because what she worried about most was about to happen and she wouldn't have to live with the guilt anymore. She made the decision to stay put and let this car accident be her final act. Drop the curtain.

Kill the guilt. Kill the pain. Kill the memories.

CHAPTER 2

Claire's home - South Dakota – June 1993

"Mom!" Josie said desperately, her shriek breaking the peacefulness of the golden hour as it filtered through their kitchen window and highlighted Claire's soap-and-water glistened hands. "Mom I need you!"

A moment later, "MOM!" Her voice was cracked and broken. So unlike the sensible, reserved teenager, Claire knew instantly that something was terribly wrong. It wasn't a spider or a bat in her daughter's bedroom, as they'd had in previous years. Josie could fend for herself when it came to those critters. This was serious; her cries were desperate. *A really gigantic spider? A whole cache of bats hanging in her wardrobe? Discovery of an intruder who had been hiding in one of the spare rooms?*

Claire laughed at her own exaggerated imagination, dropped the pan she was washing in the stainless steel sink and bolted up the tiny staircase, two at a time, careful not to bang her head on the low ceiling where the stairs curved slightly in the eighty year old house. Slipping on the hardwood floors with her stocking feet, she yelped in surprise, caught herself on the bedroom door jam and swung around with her head poking into the doorway as she said, "What's wrong?"

Sitting on the edge of her full sized bed, complete with it's matching gray and teal pin-striped pillowcases and sheets - Josie's request as one of her few Christmas gifts several years ago - was her panic-stricken faced daughter holding a home pregnancy test stick in her trembling hands. The dark haired seventeen year old looked wide-eyed, shocked, as if someone had just thrust a dagger into her chest and she was waiting for the pain to hit so she could use her last breath to scream. Tears were streaming down the girl's face as Claire struggled to comprehend the scene before her.

"What?" Claire asked breathlessly, wiping her wet hands on her jeans. "What is that? What's going on?" She stepped further into the room, craning her neck to confirm what Josie was holding. "What is that Josie?" Her voice more shrill.

The girl held the stick up toward her mother so the little pink plus sign was visible.

"I'm pregnant," Josie managed to squeak out between sobs. Her shoulders rocking under the weight of her disbelief.

A dreamlike trance came over Claire as if she were viewing this scene on a movie screen through a sepia toned filter and a thick layer of haze. *It couldn't be. Not my Josie. Not her youth group attending, popular honor student, MVP of the volleyball team two years running, doer of all things good, daughter. Pregnant?* Surely Claire didn't hear correctly.

"What are you talking about?" She stepped forward, grabbing the test stick and seeing for herself the small pink plus sign in the indicator window. Feeling like she'd been sucker-punched in the gut and now unable to breathe, she stepped back and leaned against the door jam, dropping the stick to the ground as if it were scalding her fingers.

She could hear her daughter sobbing and what sounded like a freight train running through her brain. *Pregnant? What? How?* She shook her head furiously back and forth trying to make sense of the nightmare just presented to her. *No way. Not MY Josephine Kay.*

Her chest grew tighter as the anger blossomed. Like boiling water brewing from the depths of a geyser, Claire felt herself being consumed by rage unlike anything she'd experienced before. It began in her feet and made its way up her body, warming her skin as it crept along. It was consistent and thorough, not slowing down even one bit when it encircled her heart, before presenting itself through her face.

Glaring at her daughter she hissed in anger, "What have you done?"

Josie coiled back, as if that same boiling water had just been thrown on her. "N... n.. nothing mom. It wasn't my fault," she said, shaking her head and retreating to the center of the bed, her knees drawn to her chest, subconsciously protecting herself from the blows.

"Oh really?" Claire's sarcasm raised her voice a few notches, her breathing quicker now as her pulse began to race. "A girl doesn't just get pregnant like that." She snapped her fingers. "Overnight and without fault." Her mind reeled as she imagined all the times Josie had spent the night at her best friend Sara's house and how that left ample opportunity for lies to be told and evenings to be spent elsewhere.

Would a girl like Sara lie about Josie's whereabouts though? The two girls were the same age and had been best friends since Kindergarten. They grew up having countless sleepovers, playing together in the high school band and in various sports, attending church and youth group weekly. Sara's father was a Gideon and leader of their church. *Surely his daughter wouldn't lie for mine. Would she?*

But then again, she'd never been that impressed with that man's insistence to share his faith with anyone who was within earshot, be it at a volleyball game, band concert, grocery store or middle of a gravel road if he were so lucky as to encounter someone out there while tending to his cattle. Sure, he helped supply area hotels and strangers with Bibles, which is all good and fine, but to push your religion into the faces of everyone around you? It seemed a bit presumptuous to Claire. Even Josie had mentioned that the man made her and Sara do devotionals after supper when Josie was there at sleepovers. Not really the kind of thing teenagers want to be doing at any given time.

"Stop lying to me Josie. Girls just don't show up pregnant by doing nothing." Claire seethed through clenched teeth.

Maybe she'd been at that boy Nick's house. His mother Diane turned into such a lush the last couple of years. Drinking at the bar when Nick and her husband were at home. Heard she got fired from another job just last week.

"I didn't do anything wrong." Josie, defeated and broken, whispered between sobs. Her shoulders fell forward in obvious defeat.

"Is it that boy Nick? Did he do this to you?"

Josie's eyes widened as she dared look at her mother, her breath caught mid-sob as she started to comprehend what her mother was implying. "No. It wasn't him. It wasn't anything I did. I..."

"I don't believe you." She shrugged, crossing her arms in defiance. The silence was roaring; the tension between them solid and heavy, like a headstone sinking into newly cultivated earth. Claire's mind ran rampant with fictitious scenarios of how and when and with whom, Josie had been messing around with. She clenched her fists to keep from hitting the walls.

"So you think you're some big high school graduate now and don't need to mind my rules, or... or..." The anger was taking over. "Or behave anymore?"

Josie sat wide-eyed at her normally rational, albeit very judgmental and impatient mother, now out of control with false assumptions.

"So you've been going to parties behind my back and having sex with random boys? Is that it?" She paced the room between the dresser and door leading to the narrow hallway. "Or screwing Nick while his mother is passed out on the couch?"

A mortified expression covered Josie's face as Claire imagined her daughter slutting herself around school with random boys. *And look where that landed her... just out of high school and pregnant.* "So while I'm at work every night, putting food on our table and clothes on your back and a roof over your head, you're out having sex and lying to me?!" Her voice was high and loud, a stark contrast to her normal calm, peaceful voice.

How dare she do this to me! It took over fifteen years to build a respectable life in this place and now it's going to be ruined by my own flesh and blood.

Josie's mouth was agape, the crying ceased because of her mother's horrible accusations. She was a Christian, an Honor Roll student, National Honor Society member and Salutatorian of her graduating class at East Valley High School. She was a starting volleyball player, the MVP and co-captain of the team, President of the Drama Club and had never gotten a detention at school or a grounding at home in all her years.

She'd never even been kissed by a boy until the summer before her Junior year of high school and that was by Nick, her current and steady boyfriend for the past two and a half years. Yes, his mother drank too much as of lately, but that didn't mean Nick was to blame or acted in defiance to compensate for her misgivings. Josie knew that she and Nick had a solid relationship built on trust and a long standing friendship with commitments to remain celibate until marriage, should they be so blessed to enter into that together.

"No... n... no, Mom. I haven't done anything like that." She was shaking her head back and forth feverishly. Certainly her mother would give her the benefit of the doubt. Josie had never given cause for her mother to worry about her whereabouts or actions. She gathered what energy she had left to defend her case.

"I was raped." she said softly but firmly.

Claire stood still for a long moment, staring at the girl, then bristled her back and brought her chin up.

"Raped?" she rasped.

Josie nodded her head, reddened eyes wide in fear but also expected anticipation of her mother's support and sympathy.

"Raped?" More matter of fact this time, hands moving to her hips. "That's the story you're going with, huh? You galavant around behind my back and get knocked up and that's the story you're going with?" Sarcasm oozed from her mouth like saliva as her hands flew through the air as if playing charades with her spoken words.

Josie could only stare in disbelief. Who was this woman before her? She knew her mother could be judgmental, petty and vain, criticizing others on a daily basis for anything from their clothes to how many times they'd been divorced. But despite that, she was normally a good woman who was constantly volunteering at church for one thing or another, and working extra hours at the hospital to cover shifts for those out sick or on vacation.

Josie had also known her mother to be a strict enforcer of manners and rules when raising Josie, but it led to Josie's work ethic, determination and ambition to succeed. Up until this very moment the two women had been fairly close. They had to be, they were all the other had. No more family in the area, save for her dad's parents in Omaha whom they saw a few times a year. So the two women relied on each other for company in the evenings, when Claire wasn't working, for conversations about school and work, an occasional movie and even some gossip now and then. How, now, could she be so accusing and horribly mean?

Claire was furious, sweat beaded across her forehead and she clenched her hands until her knuckles were white just to prevent them from shaking. "So if you were raped then why didn't you tell me or the police about it when it happened? I mean, how dumb do you have to be to hide something like that?"

She didn't stop the painful words from spewing out, and it shocked Josie at how little her mother cared about her in her most desperate of moments. Josie could feel her heart begin to close off.

"You know what?" Claire said, throwing her hands up in surrender before the stunned girl had a chance to speak. "It doesn't matter how, when or where this shit happened, the bottom line is I'll be damned if I let a child ruin your life like it did mine." She pointed a stern finger at Josie's face. "You are *not* keeping this baby."

With that she stormed out of the room, slamming the thin door behind her, shaking a chunk of plaster loose from the lathe beneath. It cracked into several pieces as it landed on the wooden floor under Josie's windowsill.

CHAPTER 3

The James River – July 2005

Claire had taken one deep, final breath when the water floated her to the ceiling of the car, forcing the last bit of oxygen either into her lungs or out the broken window, but with the intensity of the situation she couldn't remember how long ago that was. Was she nearing her three minute mark? Or was it closer to five?

Claire grimaced against the warm water, trying to writhe away from the painful memories of that fateful night when her world came crashing down from its pinnacle and her relationship with Josie was all but destroyed. A sob escaped her mouth, the bubble of air smashed and silenced by her soon to be metal coffin. Tears meant nothing in the watery grave. They were unnoticed and swept away in the river to join the flow of countless other tears that rolled off someone's pain stricken face.

She could feel the darkness closing around her like a shroud of black ink poured from an inkwell. Her body tingled from an unknown chill; her lungs burned and pricked from lack of oxygen. With muddled and distant thoughts, she recognized a glimmer of gratefulness at finally getting a reprieve from her guilty conscience. After all these years she could finally stop thinking about it.

Through squinted, tired eyes, just before the blackness enveloped her, beyond the silt floating aimlessly before her, she saw the cracked windshield lit up by the soft glow of the dashboard lights. *They still work under water? Weird.*

CHAPTER 4

The In-between Place

Darkness slowly faded to light, like the coming of a fog-wrapped sunrise, as Claire rose into consciousness, level by level like a slow elevator rising skyward from the basement of a high-rise building. From behind closed lids she could see the sunlight and feel its warmth on her skin. The breeze made nearby cottonwood tree leaves sound like a million tiny pairs of hands clapping with delight. It was one of Claire's favorite sounds and she recognized it instantly.

Underneath her outstretched body was something soft and cool that conformed to her body's every curve and length. It was the earth in some form, beckoning her to stay and rest in its embrace. Birds were chirping incessantly from all directions, having mini conversations about feathered avionics techniques or nest building strategies and she wondered, if translated to English, how intriguing their words would be.

She had perfect peace. No pain or discomfort. No untamed thoughts or worries or sense of urgency to do anything but breathe. And so she lay there for long, drawn-out minutes, basking in the glory of the most wonderful sense of reverence she'd ever known.

Curiosity eventually got the best of her and she summoned her mind to move her body. To ensure she was able-bodied she forced her hand to move and then her arm, shifting them just enough to feel her tank top and cotton shorts. *Dry? How can that be?* She wiggled both feet to ensure their mobility, testing her other hand now and bringing it up to her face. Touching her dry hair, loose around her shoulders. Her nose, lips and closed eyelids were inspected and she was relieved to feel she was intact. No injuries, near as she could tell. Nothing hurt at least. *How did I get out of the car and onto the shore? And why is it light out? Have I been outside all night?*

Unable to resist any longer, she slowly opened her eyes, peeking through her parted eyelids.

A touchable blue sky, brilliant and sparkling like a trillion baby blue diamonds greeted her. Cotton-ball shaped clouds floated along, their individual journeys dictated by the breeze. Their texture was visually surreal, like oil paint on canvas. Rich and thick and almost creamy looking. Cirrus clouds, higher above in the atmosphere, ebbed and flowed to their own resonance; the wispy ringlets alive with movement, rippling first left, then right, as if playing a virtual game of catch-me-if-you-can with each other.

Searching for the sun so she could turn her face fully toward its warmth, she examined the sky for the bright spot that would reveal its location, but found none specific to such criteria. Such did the light so illuminate the sky that the sun seemed hidden behind every cloud. It was everywhere and nowhere simultaneously.

You're not in Kansas anymore, she thought, smiling to herself at the quote from one of her favorite movies. *Or maybe not even South Dakota anymore.* This certainly wasn't any place she recognized. It was far more beautiful than anything on the earth as she knew it.

Claire pushed herself into a sitting position, stretching her legs before her. The James River, or "The Jim" as locals called it, lay in front of her, the familiar landmark bridge was above her to her left, its gray cement railing no longer matte and bland but rather glistening like polished rock under the sunlight. Normally the river was four to nine feet deep in any given location, just deep enough to provide refuge for catfish and smallmouth bass in its brown murkiness, but now it was neither brown nor murky.

Before her was a crystal clear, barely-there shade of blue branch of water slowly flowing southward. Rounded stones lined the bottom and fish were visible; their silver glinted bodies darting about chasing one another or shadows. The water sparkled like rhinestones, reflecting the warm sun above and appeared to pulse, like lifeblood, as it brushed against the banks and passed over the rocky bottom.

Thick-trunked cottonwood trees towered over the river's edges, hovering over the more petite mountain ash, willows and boxelders. The vibrant, green-hued leaves looked soft to touch, like plush velvet and suede or short-napped faux fur. They fluttered in the breeze; an endless applause of life and princess-like elbow-and-wrist waves to an unseen audience. Lilac bushes laden with clusters of blooms, displayed their lavender opulence proudly against the green of the foliage.

Underneath her lay the softest bed of grass she'd ever had the privilege of sitting on. She sank into it and it hugged every curve of her body. Upon touching it she discovered it felt alive, moving of its own accord in harmony with the breeze and movements of the earth beneath it into which it dug its life-giving roots. It was so divine she felt guilty for squishing it down with her body weight.

She gingerly got to her feet and noted she was wearing the same khaki shorts and white tank top from the night before but they were spotlessly clean, not stained from the dingy river water and sludge that covered the bottom of the Jim. Tip-toeing to the water's edge she peered at her reflection. Her long brown hair was neat and hanging straight down her back; shiny with every strand still in place. Both silver hooped earrings were intact and accounted for. Her dark gray manicured nails were impeccable. Relief flooded her knowing she wasn't mangled, but rather she looked healthy with rosy cheeks and a youthful glow that she hadn't known since her twenties. *Nice.*

But there's no way I got out of that car uninjured. Maybe this isn't The Jim. Too pretty. Way too clear. Where am I?

Turning in a full circle she scanned the river bottom hills. Brome, Indian and switchgrass blanketed the hillsides and swayed to and fro like orchestrated performers promenading about on nature's stage. The hills themselves were speckled with the usual cedar trees, from the newly emerged to the mature specimens, but instead of being a dark, dull shade of olive green, they were vivid, almost glowing. Their blue seeds clustered on the branches like tiny grapes ready to be picked by the birds and distributed in their unique forms and fashions.

Purple phlox and pointed thistle, yellow yarrow, pasque, black eyed Susans, milkweed and brightly colored dandelions peppered the countryside. Their respective colors, shimmering like gems and sequins not normal petals, seemed to float off the flowers as though they didn't belong there in the first place. Bumble bees the size of almonds skirted about obtaining and disbursing pollen amongst the flowers while Monarch butterflies fluttered nearby, taking their turn at the sweet nectar.

Ravines ran up the sides of the valley, wrinkles in the landscape, ushering rain water down from the uplands and feeding the river that ran through its midsection. Its presence cutting a gorge through farmable land and prime whitetail habitat. She saw them now, the deer, stopping to graze on the dense grass as they ambled across the valley; the males displaying their trophy antlers to prospective female partners. A trio of rabbits and a fox tended their daily commissions side-by-side while a pair of red tail hawks and a bald eagle observed from above, their mission that of protectors rather than hunters.

She turned again, looking for the valley's familiar landmarks. The Stone Church, three-quarters of a mile across the valley, with its rough hewn walls constructed from split field rocks. The old Osterman farm just across the highway from the church nestled into a crook of the river. The new house Jack and Gail Rickson had built to the northwest of the church, up on the hillside, a few years back. A mile down the road to the east, a set of twin silo tops were normally visible next to the roof line of a large white barn.

But today there was nothing. No church. No farms, houses or silos. Even the row-crop fields were merely meadows now; dazzling displays of wildflowers and wildlife. Waist-high prairie grass flowed in the breeze like the waves of the ocean at high tide. The valley looked nearly the same, save for the exuberant colors and textures, but there was no evidence of anything man-made except the bridge where she had crashed after nearly hitting that boy.

The boy!

She had forgotten about him. Last night while driving home from work, and nearly there, he suddenly appeared on the road right in front of her car. Swerving to miss him, her car had flipped over the bridge railing, then somersaulted before landing upright in the dark waters below.

Had the boy been fishing on the bridge? At night though? That's dangerous for an adult to do after dark, much less a child. Maybe he was here with a parent and that's who pulled me out of the car? But... where are they now?

Claire shook her head in bewilderment. *But this doesn't look like the same valley I was in last night. Maybe this is Heaven? Or a friendly version of hell; like the receptionist area before they usher you to your specific area of eternal torture.*

She rubbed her temples and ran her hands through her hair, racking her brain to figure out what was going on. Turning her head from side to side, she once again scanned her surroundings; slowly this time.

Then she saw him. The boy from the road. He wore the same denim shorts and a white t-shirt and was standing barefoot on the riverbank about a hundred yards upstream from her, his short dark hair ruffled by the breeze as he concentrated on securing his red and white bobber. She watched him cast a fishing line into the river with ease and guessed him to be about eleven or twelve.

As she waved her arms to get his attention, she hollered, "Hello!"

Over the soft grass she walked toward him, stopping once to revel in the way the landscape around her seemed to ebb and flow with each move she made as if reacting with respectful admiration to her movements. The grass and flowers leaned toward her, the breeze tickled her nose and swirled her hair about her face as if in greeting. Birds dipped out of the sky to within a few feet of her, tweeting their chorus of notes in harmony with the next.

Making her way past a cluster of large and small trees, she stopped in a small clearing of sandy ground that sloped toward the water, where a navy blue tackle box lay open on top of a knee-high tree stump, and watched the boy reel in his line. He turned to her and smiled as he walked toward her. The closer he came, the more the breeze increased as if it were coming with him; the tree leaves clapped louder and the flowers stood taller. A virtual 'hail all who pass' salute to the child.

Three wrens swooped down out of a tree, twirling in unison above his head momentarily before jetting away. A wave of unanticipated excitement ran up Claire's spine at the approaching child.

His green eyes lit up. His big grin pushed out his lightly freckled round cheeks.

"Hi Grandma," he said.

CHAPTER 5

Claire's smile quickly faded. Her eyes narrowed and she instinctively stepped back.

"Um... excuse me?" She uttered, shaking her head in disagreement. "I...um. I think you're mistaken, I'm nobody's grandma." Her voice faltered. Touching her hand to her chest, she leaned forward to speak on his level. "My name is Claire and I live down the... um, the road a few miles from here." She snapped her fingers, as if doing so would snap her out of her confusion of not seeing a road anywhere, and pointed eastward. "I was in a car accident last night and I'm... I'm looking for some help."

"Yes, I know who you are Claire. And you *are* my grandma, you just didn't know it until now." He said, reaching out his hand to introduce himself. "It's nice to finally meet you," he offered.

Ignoring his hand, she stepped back further, putting more than the tackle box and tree stump between them. She tucked her hair behind her ears, raised her chin and looked down her nose at him. "That's ridiculous. Stupid even. I don't have any grandchildren." Her breath became shallow as her blood pressure rose.

She brushed him off with a wave of her hand and turned to walk away then remembered that he was the only other person here who might know what was going on, where they were and why there weren't any buildings or roads in sight. Stopping in her tracks mere strides away, she took a deep breath before turning back around. The boy leaned his fishing pole against the stump then smiled at her once again. She hated to admit it, if even in her mind, but he sure was a handsome boy with his dark hair, kind eyes and mischievous grin. And that spattering of freckles across the bridge of his nose would be adorable if she weren't so flustered.

Back in reality, if it could still be considered that, her mind reeled as she looked around, avoiding the boy's gaze. *This is dumb. Has to be a dream. It can't be real. I'm either dreaming or I'm dead, that's what's going on here.* She pinched her left forearm - hard - and winced in pain, staring at the red mark left behind. *That felt very real.* She wiggled her bare toes; the ground beneath her feet was cool and cushioned with no stray twigs, leaves or fallen logs to hinder its perfect canopy over the river bank. She witnessed no bugs or nuisances buzzing around her or crawling on the ground. The breeze carried the smell of lilacs along its path as it wafted past her, ruffling her long dark hair and causing her to put her nose in the air and inhale deeply of that familiar smell she so loved.

I don't think I've got much of a choice here. She sighed heavily, looking at him. "Okay, so what's your name then?" Cocking her head to the side, she planted her hands on her hips. If this was some twisted kids' game, she'd play it.

"I don't have a name." He replied, shrugging and casually putting his hands in his pockets.

"Oh, of course not." She muttered under her breath. "Okay. Why not?" she said sarcastically.

"Because I was never born, so nobody gave me a name."

Claire inhaled sharply, certain that her heart stopped beating for a few seconds while she tried to grasp what he was implying. *There's no possible way that this boy was... No. Can't be. Impossible.* She vigorously shook her head in conjunction with the thoughts rambling through her brain. *He looks to be about twelve years old. Twelve years... the number of years since...*

The unpleasant thoughts quickly got pushed aside and instead she let the anger emerge. She knew how to deal with that emotion better than remorse or doubt.

"Is this some kind of sick joke?" Shaking her finger at him. "Who put you up to this?" When he didn't answer her she tried to distract herself by turning in a full circle, willing herself to see something she hadn't noticed before. A car, a road, a building, an airplane flying overhead, something to indicate she was still alive and in familiar surroundings, but there wasn't anything but nature and its creatures, the valley, the bridge and the river. And this boy. This dark haired boy whom she couldn't help but notice had the same eyes as her daughter Josephine; green with a dark circle around the outside of the cornea. She knew them well having viewed them in her own mirror for the past forty-seven years.

"I don't have time for this." She laughed at her own rationale. *You wanted to end your life in the river just a handful of hours ago and now you're complaining that you don't have time?* She was on a detour to this gorgeous, perfect, shimmering place with no foreseeable way out and she was in a hurry? The irony was beyond surreal and she quietly chastised herself for the stupidity of it all.

"This is just so dumb; I don't wanna be here. Can I go now? Can I wake up? How do I wake up and get home?" she huffed, rolling her eyes in frustration and slapping her palms on her cheeks.

The boy giggled.

Anxiety pricked at the backs of her arms and her neck and she could feel her heart beating against her chest. She gathered her long hair together, pulling it up and off her neck, fanning herself with her free hand. *I need to get out of here before I have a full on panic attack.*

The child wasn't phased. "I know it's a little weird being here and meeting me." He waited for a reply that never came.

"Try to relax, it'll make more sense in a little while," he continued.

They stood in silence for a long minute, the chirping of the birds the only sound on the breeze. He, the mysterious boy who appeared out of nowhere and she, the impatient adult who was so flustered she couldn't formulate a coherent thought.

"So, what is this place?" she finally said, desperate to fill the silence and give herself time to think of what she could do to get away from this child. "Heaven?" She cringed and uttered under her breath, "Hell?"

"Nope." The boy giggled again. "Relax. You're not dead, Grandma, you're just taking a little break."

"Oh, well thank you. That clears everything up nicely." She shook her head and began rubbing her temples even though she didn't have a headache.

"You can call me by a name if that helps you." He said, shrugging his shoulders. "Pick a name, anything is fine with me."

Claire massaged the back of her neck, buying time as she continued to sort through the confusion in her mind. *What the hell is going on?* Shaking her head with closed eyes. "This has got to be a joke. This isn't real. Right?" She aggressively slapped her cheeks this time. "I'm hallucinating or something." Her continued slapping made her wince and the boy grinned.

"Stop hurting yourself Grandma. It's actually very real." He said, swinging his arms by his sides and motioning around them. "Isn't it pretty here?"

She nodded, inhaling the abundantly fresh air that seemed to deliver invisible peace to her heart with every breath she took.

"How about you call me Jacob?" he offered. "It's a nice boy's name. Is that okay with you?" Claire was still nodding her head, convinced she was either dead or dreaming and hopeful this strange encounter would be over shortly and she could return to her normal, boring, lonely life.

"I'm glad we're here together Grandma. I've been wanting to talk to you about some things."

She snapped out of her stupor. "What things?" A tinge of anger clung to her words as her defenses rose.

"Stuff about you. Stuff about Josie."

"How do you know about her?" She felt the anxiety roll up through her body and lodge in her throat.

"God told me. And He told me He's been trying to get your attention for a very long time." Jacob said. "He has something for you."

"Oh yeah? Hmm." She didn't hide the sarcasm this time. "So what is this? God sent me here to talk about Josie and… and have you tell me what a… a horrible mother I've been to her? Or what a shitty person I am?"

His kind eyes never wavered from hers. "Nope. That's not what He has in mind."

Frustration shook through her body at his inability, or unwillingness, to answer her questions logically. "Is this an intervention for single moms on the verge of suicide?"

The boy shook his head in response to her rant. Calmness and understanding showing on his face.

Disgruntled, she continued, "You think you can just drag me along on your little mind games and... and, not think it's a big deal or a waste of my time? I don't work that way, young man. I work a lot and I work hard for my kid and myself and I take care of things. By myself!" She paused to breathe; pulse pounding in her temples. The shock of her outburst surprised even herself.

The young boy nodded his head in agreement to her statement, motioning for her to sit down on the tree stump but she refused, glaring at him in anger. "And calling me 'Grandma'? What the hell is that all about? You think you know me? You think you know what kind of life I've had and what I've had to deal with since I was a kid? You think it's been easy for me with all the crap that's happened to me?"

His calm, soft voice replied, "I don't know everything you've gone through but you sound overwhelmed with anger and sadness and I'm sorry to hear that, Grandma."

"Stop calling me that!" she practically screamed at him but he didn't flinch at the shrill tone of her voice.

His peaceful look never wavered as he closed his eyes, turning his face toward the sky. The boy's gentle disposition and his seeming communication with an unseen entity shook her into silence. *Was he praying? Worshiping?*

A brooding sort of sadness fell over her. *Oh, to have that kind of peace.* She thought about God. She felt in her heart that He didn't like her; that He'd turned His back on her many years ago and left her to the wolves. That's where the pain of death seemed more enticing than living with the pain of regret and loss, and where she thought she'd find the most peace. It certainly wasn't on this earth, in her home, church or heart.

After a full minute of stillness he finally spoke. "God has a plan for you Claire. He has a gift that He's been wanting to give you." He smiled, clasping his hands to his chest in celebration at what he'd just learned. "Something wonderful!"

She rolled her eyes.
"God would like to show you something." he said.

CHAPTER 6

The Stone Church - South Dakota - Summer 1985

He touched her arm before she could react and the space around them went black momentarily before reappearing. Astounded, Claire discovered they were standing on the lawn outside Claire's home church. The Stone Church, as locals called it. Considering it was covered in stones gathered from the valley and area fields and split by hand, the nickname was most appropriate. It towered above them, a beloved landmark in the fertile river valley, its Sunday morning shadow falling westward, touching the corn stalks in the neighboring field. It was first built in 1948 with the help of the then congregation, local masons and carpenters, and was located in the river-bottom across the valley from the bridge where she'd nearly hit the boy. Seeing it now reminded Claire of the first time she viewed the structure and how it reminded her of a majestic castle nestled in the lush valley.

Vehicles, dust-covered from driving the country roads leading to the stone structure, filled the gravel parking lot and lined up like sardines on the edge of the two-lane highway indicating to Claire that the pews were packed full of church members. A two foot high row of sandbags formed a barrier between the parking lot and the corn field to the south, remnants of the early spring flooding that occurred that year, and many other years before and since then, when the winter snows melted in northern South Dakota and flowed rapidly southward, overflowing riverbanks and disrupting life in the valley. The water that spring hadn't been terribly bad, only reaching the edge of the parking lot. In other years it had come to within six feet of the church doors, causing the congregation and local neighbors to work long, hard days until a barricade could be built, preventing the water from overtaking the old building. God had been gracious, always holding back the water far enough to spare the historical structure.

"Is that my old Delta 88?" She commented, noticing the light blue, four-door Oldsmobile parked amongst the vehicles. Her mind fumbled, seeing the car that had been in the junkyard for more than a decade. "What's going on here kid?" *Did we just time travel?*

Jacob remained quiet and led Claire across the freshly mowed lawn and through the front doors. The solid oak doors, framed with wrought iron trim and boasting twelve inch tall tarnished brass handles, made a resounding *bang* when closed. None of the people inside the church turned with the noise or acknowledged their presence in any way, giving Claire such alarm that she stopped and waved her hand directly in front of a man who happened to be standing at the back of the church serving as an usher.

"They can't see us or hear us." Jacob said as they watched the congregation finish the final hymn and seat themselves while the usher excused them, row by row. "That's how it works here."

Claire's mind struggled to comprehend where she was; in what time and space or dimension. Still not one hundred percent sure she wasn't already dead or in some kind of hallucination-filled coma. She squeezed the bridge of her nose and closed her eyes, momentarily dizzy.

Jacob noticed her reaction and patted her on the back. "You still gotta breathe, Claire." He laughed. "That part hasn't changed."

Giving him a sideways glare, Claire didn't appreciate the young child's sense of humor, especially at her expense. Forcing herself to take a deep breath, she let it out in a whoosh and stretched her neck side to side to loosen her tight muscles.

As the congregation exited the sanctuary, they lined up to shake Pastor Melvin's hand and greet the tall, sixty-something year old gentleman who had presided over their little church for the past eighteen years. The ritual was not unlike baby ducks lined up behind their mother as they waited their turn to enter a pond and was a great way for the pastor to keep tabs on his parishioners each week, warmly greeting those in attendance and tallying who, by the appearance of their facial expression and body language, might need counsel, extra encouragement or prayer.

The members chatted briskly about such a fine summer morning, the crops and how well they were growing in the neighboring fields, and asked one another about family matters and prayer requests. Their camaraderie and candid conversations mingled together with children laughing and tugging on their parent's shirt sleeves, asking to be excused to run outside until it was time to go home.

Claire saw Josie in the line, alone and quiet and probably just eleven years old. It was so strange to see her daughter that young again and Claire couldn't help but marvel at how pretty she was even then with her long hair pulled back into a french braid. Josie was clenching her church sweater, the white one with pearl buttons, tightly in her hands, and Claire, in mild confusion, wondered if there had ever been a time when Josie had gone to church without her.

Then from the corner of her eye she caught a glimpse of herself, odd as it was to watch herself in this place, wherever they were, jetting to the front of the church instead of lining up with her daughter and the other members in the greeting line. She watched her younger self, slightly thinner than she was now, stop by a mirror hanging in the stairwell to check her reflection. Dabbing at her eye makeup with the tip of her finger, then running long fingers through her hair, smoothing it before tucking it behind her ear. She straightened her skirt and was off again, down the steps to gather an armload of small boxes from the Sunday school room off to the side of the kitchen then head back upstairs. Claire noticed Josie was looking around for her and, finding her scampering around, sighed heavily and shuffled her feet awkwardly as she inched toward the pastor.

Claire watched herself go to the church's small library and set the boxes down. "If Rachel would do her job properly I wouldn't have this mess." she said under her breath, aggressively putting some of the box contents on the shelves labeled "Christian Theology" and "Children's Books". "Having five kids under the age of eight isn't an excuse to neglect her job."

The empty boxes went with her back down the steps and outside to the dumpster, at the opposite end of the church, and on her way there she walked right by dozens of church members who were gathering outside to enjoy the fresh air. Including Rachel. "Hey Rachel." she said, waving at the young blonde woman. *Should I tell her to buy a larger dress size? That thing does nothing for her rolls.* "I put those books away for you."

"Oh thanks Claire. You know, I've been meaning to do that and just didn't get around to it." A toddler yanked on her skirt, exposing her slip and nylons beneath. Frantically grabbing for her clothing, she laughed. "Oh my. Now stop that kiddo."

Claire bit her lip to keep from laughing at the scene playing out before her. She remembered that morning quite well, with Rachel's near-miss at flashing the entire church congregation. One look at Jacob's serious face brought her back to sobriety.

"Yea, well, I just took care of it for you cuz I was tired of tripping over those boxes in the Sunday school room."

Rachel paid her no mind, being distracted by three of her five children at once.

Stepping forward so as to be in Rachel's personal space, Claire continued, "You know, there's not much room in there for the Sunday school kids so any extra stuff laying around isn't okay. So next time we receive a shipment of books could you please get them put away right away?"

Without waiting for a reply from the wide-eyed woman, Claire strode away, giving an exasperated sigh. "I shouldn't have to babysit these women," she said under her breath.

Claire watched herself as she made two more stops, in different areas of the basement, to do menial tasks of which, at this point in time, Claire couldn't seem to recall what importance they were. She whizzed by fellow congregants who sat at tables or stood in small groups drinking coffee and enjoying a cookie or brownie, only to stop, once again, at the stairwell mirror to pat down her slightly wind-blown hair.

A younger woman named Kari, with bobbed curly hair and a cute purple tunic on, attempted to stop Claire. "Good morning." Kari smiled warmly, which Claire practically rolled her eyes at in her haste. "I have some questions about Bible School, do you have time to talk about it for a couple minutes?"

Out of breath from her scurrying around, Claire said, "Oh, I don't actually. I have a few things I need to get done before I leave. Can we just talk about it on the phone later this week?"

"It'll just take two minutes and I really need to show you some things in person, so it's not really a phone thing." Kari insisted.

"Okay, um, sure." she said, glancing around nervously, as if she was missing something by standing still.

As they walked toward the far classroom Claire's neighbor Dee Brown called to her. "Claire, good morning! Can I get you a cup of coffee?" Dee and her husband Rick lived a mile to the west of Claire's place, along the same river road, but despite the near vicinity of their properties, they hardly saw each other.

"Yea, it'd be nice to catch up with you, neighbor." Rick chided and gave her a big smile.

"Hi you two." Claire said, waving a dismissive hand in their direction. "I'd love to visit but I've got some things to take care of."

"Can't it wait until after a cup of coffee? We never get to see you it seems." Dee sounded disappointed.

Claire faltered between Kari and the Bible school discussion and her well-meaning neighbors. "I know. Between work, church and my volunteering I really don't have time for anything else."

"It's okay, maybe next week you can slow down enough to have a cup with us." said Rick.

"Yea, maybe." And she was off, following Kari into the classroom.

"We could have a cup of coffee with Rick and Dee, it would be nice to visit with them. They're such a fun couple." Kari offered as they stepped into the classroom.

Taking the Bible school papers out of Kari's hands herself in order to expedite the meeting, Claire said, "Oh, no, that's fine. Let's just see what you've got here. Now, you're in charge of the crafts, right? It's hard to remember all this stuff sometimes. I'm not sure why I keep volunteering to plan and lead the entire Bible school program every year, I should just ask for help I guess." She chuckled and opened the booklet provided by the Bible school program she'd decided on this year with its zoo theme. Kari watched her in astonishment as she commandeered the meeting as if she had been the one to call it, not Kari.

"Um, yes, I'm in charge of crafts and I know you told me to follow the booklet and the ideas they give for each day's crafts," Kari continued, "but I wanted to talk to you about doing some other things. I've got some really great ideas about..."

"No, that's not what we had discussed." Claire interrupted, shaking her head vigorously. "The booklet takes it day by day and has all of the supplies needed already listed for each age group. In fact I've already bought most of the supplies so we can't change it now."

"Okay, but the ideas I have aren't things that need supplies. I was thinking that we could visit the zoo one day and..."

Speaking brashly, Claire said, "No. Nope. We can't do that. Too many kids and with the liability issues and driving all the kids there and having them all at the zoo. I mean, anything could happen and we just can't do that."

"Okay, then perhaps a video about a zoo? I found a really great documentary at the library that takes a behind-the-scenes look at a day in the life of a zookeeper." Kari offered optimistically.

"No, that's not gonna work either. We already have video segments lined up for each day. I think Mary is in charge of videos this year."

"But I could show the documentary during craft time."

"Just stick with the booklet and those crafts. It'll be best that way."

And like that Claire was off, running again to her next "very important task", walking past the pastor once again, waving distractedly at another neighbor and ignoring her daughter who stood to the side with one of her friends from school.

Standing next to Jacob, Claire avoided his gaze by looking down at her shoes; embarrassed at being exposed as so rude and abrupt.

They saw Kari walk into the hallway after gathering her Bible school paperwork off the table, just as Mary walked by.

"You okay?" Mary said.

"She goes a hundred miles an hour, I swear." Kari said. Then in response to Mary's questioning look, said, "Miss Fancy Pants."

Mary grinned, seemingly well aware of why Claire had that nickname.

"What?" Claire sounded shocked. "They call me that?"

"Apparently so," said Jacob.

"Why? Cuz I dress up for church and make an effort to look nice?" *There's nothing wrong with that.*

She straightened her shoulders and stuck her chin out. "It's not my fault they don't make more of an effort toward their appearance. There's nothing wrong with being put together."

With an exasperated look on her face Kari continued, "So yea, I just talked to her about my ideas for the zoo and that documentary I told you about and she completely shot it down. So that's disappointing."

"Oh, that's too bad. They're really good ideas too."

"Why is she so demanding? Like it has to be done her way or it's wrong?"

Mary gave Kari a knowing look and shrugged. "We all know how she is Kari. We can't change her." Mary squeezed Kari's arm and raised her eyebrows. "But we can pray for her and God can change her."

Kari took a deep breath and leaned in for a sideways hug as they walked together. "Yea. I know. Thanks for the reminder. I *will* pray for her. And maybe sneak in that documentary video when she's not looking." They giggled at the conspiracy and walked away, arm in arm.

CHAPTER 7

"Demanding, huh?" Claire said, clenching her jaw and squaring her shoulders in defense. "And yea, I *am* in a hurry. You know... I'm busy, and... and stressed out most of the time cuz of work and being a single mom, taking care of the acreage and paying the bills by myself..." She swallowed clumsily and nearly choked on her own words as tears welled up in her eyes. Blinking feverishly to ward them off, she cleared her throat and walked toward the exit, flinging her hair over her shoulder as she walked.. "I do a lot for this church. I'm constantly volunteering and working endlessly to make sure Bible School, and Sunday School for that matter, are well planned and run smoothly. I have to find teachers to cover all the classes and activities cuz it doesn't seem anyone else will do it. I help in the kitchen whenever it's needed and take my turn cleaning the church every other month..."

They had reached the church's front door but it wouldn't open. Claire stopped mid-sentence and shrunk back, looking at Jacob's perfectly peaceful expression. "What?"

"You're not the only one," he said.

Claire scowled at him. "The only one what?"

"Everyone is busy. Everyone has responsibilities that demand their attention and they get worn out. In fact most people are too tired or too busy to go to church for a couple hours each week. They ignore their most basic needs." He paused to make sure she was looking at him as he spoke. "Hearing God's word and being together with other believers."

"Well, I'm used to doing things on my own; been on my own since I was seventeen ya know. I don't need anyone else." She yanked on the handle then pushed outward, trying to escape the church. "Why won't this door open?"

Jacob put his hand over hers, pausing her once again. "The world wears us down when we're too busy. We need the Church, the people and God's word, to build us back up." He spoke slowly and methodically as though speaking to a child. "That's what the Church is all about. Coming together in Christ's name to celebrate His blessings and grace, and to keep us accountable, and to be around others who can encourage us and pray for us. We come here to find answers about life, God, His teachings and blessings."

Claire huffed and tried the door handle once again, to no avail.

'Bible trivia time." He declared abruptly, smiling at her and clapping with excitement. "Did you know that Jesus was never in a hurry?" He raised his eyebrows and waited for a response that didn't come, from a woman who was trying, as always, to run away.

"He walked, He didn't run, to get from place to place. He even slept in the boat when there was a storm all around and the disciples were freaking out." He paused to giggle at the idea. "And He often went off by Himself to pray and sometimes would walk alone or separate from the disciples for a while."

Claire pursed her lips and remained quiet, her eyes darting from the ceiling to the walls, anywhere but to the boy's eyes. *Is there a point to this?*

"He was never in a hurry but He was always right on time, to perform miracles, to talk to people, to heal them. He had perfect timing for the will of God and what He had to do before He died." Jacob moved around to the front of Claire, pausing with his hand on her forearm. "There was always a purpose for where He was and what He was doing. He focused on His relationship with God the Father, but when He was needed by the people, to do God's work, He was there. Right on time."

"Oh yea? What about Lazarus?" She countered his rationale with sarcasm. "He'd been dead for several days before Jesus got to him. His timing was a little off then, wasn't it?"

"Actually, no it wasn't. If He'd been there when Lazarus was sick, He would have healed His friend and that would have been seen as a normal thing by Jesus' followers. They'd seen Him heal many people before so they'd expect that again. But because Jesus wasn't there, and Lazarus had been dead a while, performing a miracle at that point was truly amazing! Raising His friend from the dead showed the witnesses that Jesus truly was the Son of God and was sent by God, because only God could do such a miraculous thing."

Claire's thoughts were racing. *Hmm... shut down again.* Thinking about all the times she was too busy for church, or her devotionals, God in general really, only added to the weight on her shoulders. And all the times she left her daughter alone, and what about the other church members and her rudeness? What was so important that she was too busy for well-intentioned friends or neighbors? Even those that had helped her when she was in dire straits.

Her thoughts wandered back to when she and Josie first arrived in South Dakota. Claire recalled a handful of neighbors that came by to introduce themselves, then stayed to help her paint the brooder house, fix the crooked mailbox post, trim broken branches and hang a tire swing from a very tall tree. Josie's countless hours spent on the swing over the years indicated her appreciation of it.

The people of the church were more than welcoming too, knowing her situation of being pushed into single motherhood and trying to make a go of it in a new state. Alone. The pastor had made a point to visit with her on Sundays, ensuring she and Josie were settling in. Claire's standard response was then as it is now, "We're doing great. Thank you for asking".

Something resembling remorse struck a chord inside her chest and her breath caught momentarily.

Sensing her need to process the moment but not wanting to push her, Jacob said softly. "You are constantly in a hurry Claire. A lot of time is spent rushing through each day just so you can do it all over again the next morning and you miss out on a lot of blessings. There were those in your community and church who were there for you, some that needed you and there were lots of missed opportunities where God could have used you to bless others. Mostly, Josie needed you. She still does. That's part of what God wants to show you. His timing is perfect Claire. Never early, never late."

He squeezed her hand lightly. "Let's go."

CHAPTER 8

Claire's home – Spring 1982

Jacob easily opened the heavy wooden door, much to Claire's chagrin, and they stepped into the sunshine once again. But gone was the church's lawn. Instead it was Claire's small acreage sprawled around them; the cottage, with its crisp white siding and classic hunter green trim and shingles; the brooder house with its overflowing chicken population; the corral and large barn with a lone white horse standing guard; and the very large willow tree draping over the driveway.

It was a perfect spring day, the kind you read about, where the air is crisp but the sun's warmth makes it seem like summer, with hardly a breeze to discuss. Tulips and purple iris buds were showing their colors, popping up along the hillside near the clothesline and in front of the house in raised garden beds tucked neatly under the porch railing. The birds were chirping merrily and fluttering about below the tree canopy, dipping down toward the ground, then back up again with the grace of winged ballerinas. Josie was laughing at them, putting her arms out and pretending to fly, holding her hands in the air beckoning them to either perch or carry her away.

Claire vaguely remembered that day, Josie was about eight and Claire was on a mission to thin out the groves of trees surrounding their yard, prune the ones that would stay and pick up all the loose branches that had fallen off the largest trees over the past winter. And there were a lot of them! Despite the protection of the river bottom hills from the brunt of the wind, the ice and snow build-up still did its damage and broken branches lay all over the ground amongst the weathered trees. Small sticks and arm-sized branches were strewn about with a particularly large one on top of the brooder house. Claire knew she and Josie had their work cut out for them if they were to get this done in one weekend.

"Josie, come here!" Claire shouted to her daughter. Oblivious to her mother's calling, Josie kept dancing.

"Josie!" She tried again. The child's antics continued until Josie got so turned around she fell to the ground in a dizzy pile, giggling at the birds flying overhead. Claire grabbed her by the arm and yanked her to her feet. "Josephine Kay. Quit goofing off and pay attention." Her anger was obvious and a wide-eyed little girl quickly looked down at her feet in obedience.

"We have a lot of work to do today. There's no time for being stupid." She handed Josie a five-gallon bucket. "Start picking up the smaller sticks; whatever fits into the bucket. When it's full, dump it into the pickup and go back for more. Any questions?"

Josie's head shook slightly and she quietly took the bucket to the grove east of the house where the dark lavender colored phlox grew most abundantly. Gingerly stepping amongst the flowers so as not to crush them, Josie quickly filled up the bucket and retraced her steps out of the grove, finding a nest on the ground enroute. She gently picked it up and, balancing it in her left hand while struggling to carry the overflowing bucket with her right, she went to her mother.

"Mom, look." She said with a broad smile on her innocent face, "I found a bird nest. Can I keep it? It's so neat."

Without even looking up from the ground where she herself was picking up sticks, Claire replied curtly, "No. Too many germs on those things. Put it down and get back to work."

"Oh." Dejected and tearful. "Okay. Sorry."

"And stop dawdling. This job would go much faster if you'd pick up the pace a bit." Her voice was tense and edged with anger. "It's gonna take us all day at this rate and I got a hundred other things to do around here."

"She kept that nest." Claire said to Jacob, her voice barely above a whisper as she watched herself come undone. "I found it in the brooder house later that week, tucked in the corner. Maybe she thought the chickens would put it to use or something." Her shoulders dropped slightly with remorse.

CHAPTER 9

A familiar feeling of dejection washed over Claire. "You know, I found a five dollar bill once," she explained to Jacob. "I was probably nine I suppose and my dad and I went to the grocery store alone one time. It was on the ground in the parking lot and I remember how excited I was to find it cuz back then five dollars was a lot of money. I picked it up and was going to show my dad..." Looking off in the distance she fell quiet for a moment. Remembering. "He grabbed it out of my hand and threw it back on the ground, telling me, well, yelling at me, actually, saying how disgusting it was and how many dirty people had touched it or stepped on it and 'god knows where it's been' he said. He was so mad that he made me wash my hands with bleach when we got home."

She looked down at Jacob, a tear in her eye. "He called me a stupid kid. But lesson learned." She made a check-mark motion with her finger in the air. "I sure never picked any money up off the ground again." *Or looked at my dad the same way.*

I wonder how different my life would have been had my folks been more loving and encouraging, rather than dismissive. Distant.

Her mother, Eleanor, was loving, in her own way. In a proper way. The way a proper 1950's wife and mother should be. Every morning, before Claire or her brothers would awaken, their mother was dressed to perfection in a skirt and blouse; not a hair out of place. Makeup applied just enough to enhance her natural beauty. Breakfast was always on the table, hot and ready for the growing children but Eleanor wouldn't greet them with a joyful "good morning" or "how'd you sleep?" but rather remind them, daily, to sit nice, don't take too much, their father had yet to eat and he would get the largest portion. *Funny. I don't remember seeing my mother eat breakfast. Was she just the cook and waitress, allowing the rest of us to take advantage of her generosity?*

The thought saddened Claire. *Why didn't I ever notice that?*

The rest of their mornings were usually the same. Her father would enter the room and any mindless chit-chat from the children was ceased as he proceeded to clear the rest of the breakfast food from the dishes, consume it at record speed, grab his jacket, briefcase and keys from the foyer and leave for work. No looking back. No good-bye kisses or well-wishes for the day. Then her mother would clear the table and remind the kids to make sure they had what was needed for school and state how many minutes they had before the school bus arrived at the corner, two blocks away.

She usually told them to have a good day, or behave, or listen to their teachers, or some other phrase that a proper mother should say to her children. No usual 'I love yous' or hugs though. Their home was mostly filled with distance.

CHAPTER 10

Claire's thoughts were interrupted as the space around them dipped to black momentarily then reappeared later that same day at her acreage when the sun hung low in the western sky. Claire's flannel shirt and jeans were smudged with dirt, her boots covered in spring mud. A small twig caught itself in her hair begging to be retrieved and returned to its home on the ground.

And Josie, with her mind desiring to wander, forced her body to work diligently alongside her mother. Her dirty clothes a mirror reflection of her mother's. "Mom, I was wondering if any of these trees are big enough to build a tree fort in?"

"No." She didn't even look up from her work. "I mean, the trees are big enough but we don't have any extra wood or a way to get them into a tree to build anything. Besides, it's too dangerous to be playing that high."

"Oh, okay." She relented to her mother's excuse. Then a few minutes later. "So could I maybe have a fort out here in the trees, on the ground," she motioned to the thick grove, "or in one of the barns. Like a secret place just for me." She offered, timidly, the expectation of rejection clear in her voice. "I'll take care of it."

Claire let out a sigh of frustration. "Josie, you can barely keep your room clean and you think you need another place to take care of?"

"Okay, mom. Sorry." She picked up her bucket and deposited the contents into the pickup bed, before walking behind the house. Claire and Jacob followed Josie where they witnessed her fall to her knees and break down in tears. Shoulders slumped forward, her little body shaking under the weight of her mother's painful and repeated rejections.

Jacob looked up at Claire, whose face was colorless and forlorn. Her clenched fists grasped her hair and she lowered her head in shame. All these years of hardly speaking to her daughter because of one incident, or so she thought, when in reality it had been a lifetime of smaller incidents such as this. Expectations too high for a child who just wanted to enjoy life; disregard from a mother who was too tired to be considerate of a developing mind, a tender heart.

Hindsight is so clear and she could see now how heartless she was toward her child. Josie deserved better than that. Josie, so full of love for animals and nature, so willing to help and learn but who also got distracted by pretty rocks and squirrels and fluffy clouds, whose laugh could make the birds sing louder. She deserved, at the very least, a mother who let her enjoy those things, if not a mother who participated and encouraged her light-hearted zest for life.

"I was pretty dumb, huh?" Claire said, shaking her head. "So short with her. She just wanted something to call her own and I wouldn't even slow down for that."

CHAPTER 11

The In-between Place

Claire could still hear Josie's sobs but she kept her head bowed and eyes closed tightly, avoiding the sight and protecting herself.

"I was the only one she had and I treated her like a nuisance. A hindrance. I'm so impatient." She whispered. "Can't even be nice to my own kid." *Just like my dad.*

"Yes you should have been kinder and more loving.[1] When we interact with other people we should treat them with kindness, patience, humility and compassion [2] so we can be more like Christ and follow His example. That's how we show love to others.[3] God has been very kind and loving toward us, even though we're all sinners,[4] and we're supposed to do the same thing to other people. It's just one way we can show God how much we appreciate all that He's done for us."

He touched her arm to get her attention. "But you also have to give yourself grace. Remember, you were a child trying to raise a child. A teenager, with an infant. You're not perfect [5] and you didn't have all the right answers. You had to discover them as you went along."

Claire nodded, remembering how difficult it had been to move to South Dakota with a toddler, find work, and childcare, make ends meet and all before she was twenty years old. She'd been overwhelmed with grief and depression and most days it was all she could do to function without crying constantly. Still, it didn't excuse her behavior toward Josie. She didn't need the boy to tell her that. The convictions of her heart were enough.

"Did you have anyone to help you after Alan died?"

"Let me guess. God told you about him too?" She managed a half smile for Jacob even though she tensed up, hating the idea of opening old wounds. But here, in this In-between place, it seemed okay, even safe.

"Yep." He nodded.

Claire shook her head, remembering her husband all those years ago. His handsome face, warm smile and deep brown eyes. If she closed her eyes she could still feel his strong arms around her; he gave the best hugs, not letting go until she was ready. She hadn't had a good hug since then.

She sat down on the soft grass and tipped her head back to take in the warm sunlight. "From the moment we met he was the only friend I had. I neglected my high school friends so I could be with him. Then when he went back to the Navy a few months later, my friends avoided me cuz I was pregnant. Let me tell ya, that doesn't go over well in a private catholic school. No one wanted to be associated with me." She laughed despite the painful memories.

"Wanna tell me about it?"

Claire wondered how this boy, this child, could comprehend adult issues. But then again, he claimed God told him things so perhaps he was far wiser than his years. She sat forward, wrapping her arms around her knees. "I was seventeen; a senior in high school. He was twenty and had been in the Navy for a couple years already when we met at our annual fall church festival. He was there with his cousin, who was a friend of mine from school."

Jacob listened intently. Sitting cross legged, elbows resting on his knees, chin in hand.

"He had a broken arm." She indicated to her right forearm, "From a training exercise, so he was on leave til that healed up. We got to talking, hit it off and were inseparable from then on."

"Did your folks like him?"

She laughed. "They never met him cuz I wasn't serious about him. I just wanted…"

Jacob looked at her, cocking his head to the side.

Blushing at having to admit this to a child, she continued. "Sex. Our relationship was based on sex, from my perspective at least, and since my folks were staunch Catholics who harshly frowned upon such activities, I lied to them and snuck around behind their backs to see Alan. I just figured once he returned to active duty I'd just go back to my normal life. I'd finish high school, go to college in Boston like I wanted to and get on with my career as a famous architect." She grinned at the memory of how determined she was to make it big in a big city.

She looked at Jacob with a twinkle in her eye. "I wanted to design sky-scrapers and travel the world. I wanted to get out of small-town nowhere Nebraska and away from my parents."

"But…?" he prodded.

"But I got pregnant with Josie."

Silence fell for a long minute; even the usually chattery birds seemed to wait with anticipation at the story unfolding before them.

"I was mad. Really, really mad. I didn't necessarily love Alan back then, you know. He was a nice guy and all, but… I didn't want a guy or a kid to ruin my career plans." A deep breath cleared her head enough to keep going. Funny how admitting this to the boy didn't seem to bother her. It felt good. Calming.

"I told Alan about the baby over the phone and told him I wanted to get an abortion. He freaked out and told me I couldn't do that, that he loved me and would marry me and we'd make a real good life together." She shook her head in disbelief. "He said adoption was out of the question too. Said he didn't want to live the rest of his life not knowing where his child was and if it was okay and safe and happy."

She closed her eyes and took several deep breaths to fend off the tears before continuing. "So… going back a little further, you gotta understand that my father wasn't a loving man. He worked long hours at his law firm and wasn't home much. Didn't really spend time with us kids let alone tell me that he loved me or that I was good enough or that I was pretty or anything like that. But Alan told me all those things… and, well…" Tears welled up in her eyes. "I believed him. I had longed for a man to make me feel important my whole life and there it was. Finally. And I thought if I didn't take advantage of the situation I may not ever find another guy that said those things to me. So I told myself that if I didn't love him now that I would soon enough and it'd all be okay, even if we had a kid, cuz love can overcome anything." She chuckled softly. "At least that's what young girls are led to believe."

"He told me there were colleges in Arizona, where he was stationed, that I could take architecture classes at and the military would pay for it. He wanted to see me reach my goals in life even with a baby at home. So I told my parents about the pregnancy, hoping that maybe they'd accept it, but no. They freaked out." Laughing at the painful memory after all these years was the only thing Claire knew to do, considering how things turned out.

"They kicked me out of the house and disowned me when I told them I was keeping the baby and marrying Alan. My father said that *any pregnancy outside of marriage was an abomination to the Lord and I'd burn in hell for my actions*." She lowered her voice to imitate her father's final farewell speech to his only daughter.

Jacob closed his eyes as if in prayer and reached out to hold Claire's hand. She held it tight for a few moments.

"I packed my things, called Alan and he had his dad come to our house to get me. Then I went to live with Alan's parents until I was done with high school a few months later. The day I left my house my two younger brothers were crying and my father told them to shut up and go in the house if they couldn't control themselves." A series of tears slipped down her cheeks. "They were just ten and thirteen at the time. I haven't seen them since." She whispered, emotion gripping her heart.

Jacob squeezed her hand and let the moment rest a bit before continuing. "Was your mother sad?"

"Yea. I think so. I mean, she had tears in her eyes but wasn't allowed to hug me or speak. My father stood between her and I and made sure of that. I looked her in the eye and told her that I was sorry and that I loved her so much and I saw her nod her head. My dad told me he was ashamed of me and that I was weak for giving into temptation, then they turned and left me there on the side of the street."

With her thumb she rubbed the boy's small hand. The hand that resembled her little brother's from so long ago; the ache in her heart caused her physical pain at the memory of those boys she left behind. "I tried to call our house a few times after that, when I got to Arizona, and talked to my brothers for a few minutes. I told them I was doing really good and that I loved them and to behave... and then I got my father on the phone the second time I called and he hung up on me when he heard my voice. After that they must have changed their phone number because I never could reach them again."

"That is sad. Must have been very hard for you to be away from your family."

Tears now rolled freely down her cheeks. "Yea. But that was the price I paid for my mistakes."

"Was Josie a mistake? I mean, after she was born and all?"

Claire laughed again at the loaded question. *Oh my gosh.*

"You're just a kid. Are you sure you wanna talk about this stuff?"

"I think *you* need to talk about this stuff." Came the soft reply.

Wow. Claire sighed deeply knowing the boy was right. Again. "No. Not at first, cuz I had Alan there and even though he was busy with work we still had most evenings and weekends to bond with each other and the baby and make some great memories together. And I did fall in love with him." She whispered. "Deeply. He was my best friend and treated me like a queen, always attentive and complimenting me. Such a wonderful father too. My goodness he adored his daughter." She paused to wipe tears from her cheeks. "But then he was sent to Vietnam and..."

She couldn't continue. Saying it out-loud was still too painful.

"He died?" said Jacob.

She nodded, recalling the day a priest and Naval officer rang the doorbell and informed her Alan wouldn't be coming home. That was in March of 1975, shortly before the war ended. Josie was sixteen months old and herself just nineteen when her world collapsed around her.

"I didn't know anything about raising a kid by myself and I didn't really have any friends down there; just a couple other military wives that lived near us. I wasn't allowed to stay on base after he was gone, so I called Alan's parents and they took us in for a few months after his funeral."

"So how'd you end up in South Dakota?"

"Brett, Alan's good friend from high school, lived up here with his wife and kids and I saw them at the funeral in Omaha. He told me he owned a little acreage down by the river that no one lived in. Said if I wanted to fix it up I could live there rent free for the first year, then maybe buy it if I decided to stay in the state. So that's what we did."

"Didn't you want to stay by Josie's grandparents?"

She shook her head. "Naw. I didn't feel I could stay in Omaha. Not knowing it had been Alan's old stomping grounds and the place we first met. Or knowing that my family was probably still there and most likely still hated me. Too many memories were haunting me so I moved us north and told Alan's folks where we were so they could visit, which they did several times a year when Josie was in high school. And then we started rebuilding our lives."

"Wow." he said.

"Yea, pretty wild, huh?"

Jacob nodded.

"I've always heard that God never gives us more than we can handle, but that sure didn't seem like the case back then."

"That's incorrect, actually." He looked at Claire and quickly continued before her defenses flared. "We live in a fallen world and so much of life is more than we can handle. That's where Jesus comes in. He wants to carry the burdens for us; to be our strength and shield. That's faith! By ourselves it's difficult, sometimes even impossible, but it's easy for Jesus. We just have to surrender to Him." [6, 7, 8]

She let out a long sigh as the realization that total personal responsibility for carrying the weight of her world fell off her shoulders. "Yea, I should have known that." she whispered. "All those years in church never taught me that lesson. I still felt obligated to do it all myself and I felt God was being unfair with me."

The young boy was quiet for a while. "So if you didn't rely on God, then how did you deal with all of it?"

"Work and church." she chuckled despite herself. "But seriously, I worked. A lot. Too much really cuz I was gone most of the time."

She absentmindedly twirled a strand of grass around her finger, then untwirled it. Reluctant to pluck such a perfect specimen from the lush ground.

"I loved Josie of course, but after Alan died I was so consumed with myself and grieving and just trying to survive as a single mom, that I saw her as a weight on my shoulders. Just another obligation and burden to deal with alone." She looked thoughtful for a moment as the realization of the truth hit her. "No wonder I treated her like a nuisance if that's how I felt about her in my mind." She dropped her head into her hands and choked back a sob.

"She still turned out really good." Jacob said, trying to point out the silver lining. "Cuz God was there with her even when you weren't.[9] And God was working in her life, and yours, through those circumstances." He touched her arm, causing her to look at his innocent face.

This time Claire shrugged. "I don't know. I guess she was a good kid. She never gave me any trouble, but then I truthfully hadn't paid much attention for so many years because of my work schedule and volunteer obligations, and then after the... the incident, she left for college we lost touch almost completely." Claire's gut twisted knowing *she* was the one that lost touch; it was no fault of Josie's or lack of attempting to maintain a relationship.

"Would you like to see her during those years?"

Claire nodded excitedly.

"I think you'll like this."

CHAPTER 12

East Valley High School – May 1993

Jacob reached for her hand and within seconds East Valley High School lay in front of them. Its reddish brown brick walls and black shingled roof rising up to meet the blue sky. She and Jacob were standing on the sidewalk looking across the street at the school as the last bus unloaded a dozen kids of all ages. The teenagers were just as excited as the grade schoolers as they clamored out of the bus, chatting excitedly, and made their way to the front doors. Several teachers were outside calling greetings while simultaneously urging them to stop dawdling and get inside before the final bell rang.

A tall man with an athletic sweatshirt that had "Coach Deskin" embroidered on the chest pocket hustled the last two squirrely grade school boys into the building before securing the double doors behind them. "Thank god it's the last day of school" the Coach commented to another teacher as they shared a knowing look.

As she looked around, Claire noticed a large banner hung in the main hallway above the lockers that read "Congratulations Class of 1993!!" in large hand-painted yellow and maroon letters, the school colors. It appeared that all of the underclassmen and teachers had signed it, giving the graduating class a warm sendoff. Claire held her breath for a minute processing the fact that they were at Josie's high school. On the last day of her senior year. *The day of that dreadful party by the river.*

A couple dozen students were scattered up and down the hallway cleaning out their lockers, throwing unneeded items in four strategically-placed large black garbage bins and stuffing books into already bulging backpacks, exchanging quips with their friends about their summer plans and vacations they were going on in the coming months.

Jacob proceeded down the hallway to the second room on the left. A sign beside the door said "Room 104 - Economics".

The classroom was full of what seemed to be highly caffeinated students mingling and chatting, Josie amongst them. Jacob and Claire walked closer to Josie and could overhear her talking with a friend as the bell rang. Claire recognized the girl as Kim, a classmate of Josie's who had gone to church youth group with her daughter several times.

"I wanna go to that river party tonight." Said Kim excitedly, sitting at a desk at the far back of the classroom and stretching out her long, tanned legs from beneath a too-short baby pink skirt.

"I thought you partied Saturday night after graduation?" said Josie, claiming the desk next to Kim and looking surprised.

Shifting forward in her seat, leaning toward Josie, Kim said, "I did but that was to celebrate graduation. This is the last day of our high school careers! We have to celebrate that too!"

Josie laughed nervously and shook her head, "Ummm… I don't know. I mean I thought we agreed to see that new movie in Yankton?" She looked disappointed. "I've been looking forward to it for weeks."

Rolling her eyes, Kim replied, "C'mon you pansy! We can go to that tomorrow. This could be our last chance to see some of our classmates for months or even years! We can't miss this opportunity."

"Alright class. Your attention please!" The gray-hair-dyed-medium-brown, sixty-two years old and still wearing skirts above her knee, economics teacher Mrs. Ayers, said sternly. "I know it's the last day of school and of course we're not going to do much today, but we do need to pay attention please. Let's make the most of this time together."

Josie sat straight forward, her posture impeccable. Head and chin up, ready to pay attention and listen to whatever it was that teachers talked about on a Senior's last day of high school, which couldn't be too important considering they'd already turned in their text books and taken final exams. Josie had a worried look on her face and Claire could tell her daughter was not happy with Kim changing their plans. Other kids were still talking and carrying on about where to go for their last high school lunch break and would they get wings and fries from Roosters downtown, or stay at the school cafeteria and relish one last not-nearly-enough-to-fill-a-teenager's-stomach lunch?

Josie, seizing the opportunity to continue their conversation, craned her head around toward Kim and said, "No. I don't want to go to the river. You go ahead without me Kim, it's okay. Maybe we can catch that movie later this week before it leaves town."

"We'll talk about it later." Kim whispered as the teacher raised her voice to get the class to quiet down.

"She's so pushy. My goodness." Claire said, leaning over in front of Kim, mere inches from her face, and scowling at her. "I wish she could hear me; I'd tell her that to her face. Tell her to stop being such a..."

"Claire." Jacob said. "There's something else you should see."

Claire gave Kim one final disapproving look before following Jacob out of the room and into the now empty hallway. In the distance a door slammed, most assuredly from a student running late to class. Excited chatter could be heard through several classroom doors, indicating all of the students were eager to get this day over so their summer could officially begin. It wasn't typical for school to continue past the actual day of graduation, but living in the Midwest brought weather related challenges, and therefore days where school was called off. Although the district allowed for a certain amount of snow days, if they went beyond those allotted days, then their overall school year would be extended.

That past winter had been particularly difficult with a lot of snowfall that began in late October and didn't end until a massive two-day blizzard blew through on March 2nd, leaving them with eleven more inches of heavy snow. The original last day of school should have been the prior Thursday with the seniors graduating on Saturday, as had been planned for the entire year. However, missed school days pushed them out until today, Tuesday, and seniors were required to attend or risk not getting their diplomas. All Seniors were sure to attend. The small community of 652 residents, plus or minus, kept a pretty close eye on their kids and taught the upcoming generations to be well mannered and respectful.

CHAPTER 13

The boy led them to a set of thick double doors, each with a small inset window, that led to the library. Dark brown, ceiling high shelves lined the interior walls, proudly boasting their rows of book jackets in every color imaginable. Thick, wooden tables and chairs were scattered about the room with an oversized desk to the left, in front of the children's book section.

On a couple of the tables two dozen yearbooks were laid out, each identified by a Senior's name written on a white slip of paper affixed to the front covers. This was a tradition here at East Valley - to put all of the Seniors' yearbooks in the library and those classmates, underclassmen and teachers who wished to sign their names or write a note in the books were welcome to. It was a fun way to tell each other last-minute well-wishes, or recall a fond memory, or to say goodbye.

They found Josie's yearbook and Jacob pulled out the chair, indicating Claire to sit down. "You should read some of the things people wrote in Josie's."

She glanced at him inquisitively to make sure it was okay. It almost felt like an invasion of privacy to read notes her daughter's friends had written specifically to her. Hesitantly she sat down and looked at the front cover of the book. It was gray and depicted a hand drawn image of the high school building, with a boy and girl in front of it holding hands. They both wore graduation gowns and hats and were standing on a map of the world with its continents and borders depicted in bold lines. The class motto "Follow Your Dreams Wherever They Lead You" was scripted on the front, along with "East Valley High School - 1992-1993".

Claire smiled at the drawing, knowing it was her daughter's handiwork. Josie had always loved drawing and had been on the yearbook committee since her Freshman year, writing articles and taking photos for it and the town newspaper, and designing the very book that lay in front of Claire. Josie had presented the idea to the other committee members to have a unique, never done before, cover for their yearbook and they'd readily agreed to it - with the condition that Josie be the one to draw the image. Claire recalled Josie stressing over the project for months, discarding sheet after sheet of images, and finally, after settling on her final idea, she nervously presented it to the committee who loved the concept.

Now it sat before her, her daughter's handiwork, and wondered where Josie's original dreams would have led her. Sure she went to college, but would she have excelled more? Met more friends or just different friends? Maybe went into teaching like she always wanted to do instead of psychology? That single day twelve years ago had changed so much for both of them.

Claire gingerly opened the front cover and saw a dozen or more notes written by students, some in red ink, some blue, some black. One bold student wrote "Don't forget me!" in green marker, all capital letters, with her unreadable name scribbled below it. Claire grinned painfully at the notion of forgetting friends from high school. She didn't see, speak to or stay in touch with anyone from her high school years. No one from her hometown at all actually. A pang of sadness... and was it envy?... ripped through her heart as she recalled her high school graduation day, and trying to hide her pregnant belly beneath the graduation gown. Then getting married to Alan two days later and immediately leaving for Arizona and their home on the Naval base.

Claire read every note written in Josie's yearbook from the simple, "Congratulations!" and "I'll miss you!" and "Thanks for praying for me", to the elaborate ones.

I remember how nice you were to me when I first moved here in the 4th grade! You were the only one who said 'Hello' to me my first day of school, you sat with me at lunch and even shared your milk with me when I spilled mine! (I was so scared). It's funny the things you remember, huh? But I'll never forget your kindness. I love you!! PLEASE, please let's always stay in touch. I'm gonna miss you SO much! ~Wendy

Wow! Time flies when your having fun! Your an inspiration to alot of people in our youth group and at school. You always have a smile to share and your always encoraging others. You have helped me a ton! and I'm so thankful. Have a great time in collage! ~Tony K.

Claire chuckled at the incorrect grammar of the author, Tim, and wondered if the English teacher, upon reading the entry, would correct the misspelled words in red ink.

Yo, Jesus freak. HAHA! Just kidding. You're a good person and pretty nice to talk to. Thanks for being a friend. Good luck in your future! ~Josh

This school won't be the same without you J! I wish you could be here to cheer me on my senior year but I know you'll be praying for me. You're an inspiration to so many! Seriously!! Hope you continue to make an impact in this crazy world. See ya! ~Maryanne S.

The entries went on and on, page after page. Some wrote on top of or between photos, on the margins of pages and one creative girl using purple ink wrote her note in a spiral shape the size of a coffee cup with her name crammed into the very center of the circle.

Claire's eyes welled up with tears reading about how loving and thoughtful her daughter was.

"I always thought she was like that," Claire said, admiring her daughter in written form. "That's why it's so hard to believe she'd lie to me and be so belligerent." She huffed a deep breath as Jacob lay a hand on her shoulder.

"Perhaps she wasn't lying."

Claire laughed sarcastically, pulling away from his touch as she stood. "No. I don't believe that's the case. I think people can be two different versions of themselves; one in private and one in public."

"Are you that way?" he said.

She glared at him, daring the young boy to say more. *Thinks he knows me, huh? He's just a kid.*

"It doesn't matter what these other kids wrote about Josie, that doesn't mean she didn't sneak around behind my back and lie. Sometimes good kids aren't so good when they're not being observed by teachers or parents." *Like I was when I was a teenager.* A pang of regret, or was it merely anger, ripped through her heart.

Jacob's eyes were closed, his freckled face peaceful for a moment.

Claire sighed with impatience, annoyed at how he pushed her buttons then immediately changed the subject leaving her to silently process her thoughts on the topic.

"It's time to go." he said, turning away from her.

"And maybe it was a singular mistake." she said, desperately pleading her case. "You know, a one night stand or something. Most people have at least one of those in their lifetimes."

The boy remained quiet, leading her out the door.

CHAPTER 14

They walked down the hallway as the final buzzer rang. The school day was suddenly over. Time was moving at a pace Claire couldn't comprehend; but then the twilight zone didn't necessarily adhere to common laws.

Students spilled out of every classroom and into the hallways, hollering and laughing, "Summer's here!", "We're finally done!", "Get me outta this place.", "Peace out, suckers!" The noise was overwhelming and it seemed most of the kids couldn't exit the building fast enough. Any loose papers and leftover assignments or corrected homework were thrown everywhere with no consideration for the available trash cans or for those in maintenance who would have to pick the papers up. She and Jacob watched the students for several minutes as they gathered the contents of their lockers, their gym bags and backpacks and fled the building.

"What a bunch of slobs." said Claire, turning her nose up at the teens.

Then they saw Josie at the far end of the hallway near her own locker, picking randomly thrown papers off the floor and disposing of them in a trash can. Another girl and two boys helped her. Claire recognized two of the kids from their church, the Stone Church, and knew they were in the youth group with Josie and whom she believed to be in Josie's class. *That's Allison and Chris.* Digging deep in her memory to come up with the names of Josie's classmates of whom Josie had spoken of so many years ago. The other boy was Nick, another of Josie's classmates. But not just any classmate, the two teenagers had been casually dating for the past couple of years, and as far as Claire knew her daughter really liked him. They'd been on a couple of group dates with several other kids from school to see movies, go bowling or roller skating or have a meal out, and a handful of times they'd gone out together, alone.

She and Josie were pretty close, when they actually did see each other amongst Josie's school events and Claire's work schedule, and Josie had informed her that Nick was a true gentleman. Holding doors for her, lending his jacket when she was chilled, listening intently to everything Josie said and respecting her time and talents. He was a Christian and the two youngsters had agreed to not have a physical relationship outside of holding hands and an occasional kiss. There was a reverence to their faith that they wanted to uphold until marriage, be that with one another or others.

Mr. Sutter, the 40-something, well-loved science teacher, came out of the lab and lightly reprimanded the group. "Hey you guys. No, no… you don't need to pick those up." He took several papers out of Chris's hands. "We've got this, it's okay."

"But it's such a mess Mr. Sutter." Josie said. "We just wanna help."

"Yep, and we do appreciate that." He nodded. "But this is the last day of school for you four; time to get out of here and relax a bit. Go get some ice cream. Do something fun to celebrate."

Reluctantly, but with big smiles on their faces, the four seniors picked up their belongings and bid their science teacher a good day.

"You're a great teacher Mr. Sutter!" Allison said. "Gonna miss you." The other students agreed as they turned to wave and say their goodbyes. The two young men shaking his hand in respect.

"Thanks! Good luck out there in the big world!" He called after them, a big smile in place.

Jacob and Claire followed the group outside into the bright afternoon sunshine.

Chris asked, "What are you guys doing tonight? Maybe we can grab some burgers and chislic at Meridian Corner."

"It's my little brother's birthday today so my parents are having a bunch of family over for supper tonight, so I'm stuck at home." Said Allison, disappointment etched across her face.

"We're leaving for The Black Hills in an hour for vacation so I gotta get home and pack." Nick said, stuffing his hands in his pockets.

"Figures you'd wait til the last minute to do that." Chided Josie, a smirk on her face as she rolled her eyes at him. "You're such a guy." The others laughed at his faux shock expression at the accusation.

"That's really great that your mom is taking some time off work to do that with you." Josie said with a smile.

Nick shrugged. "Well, she's in between jobs right now so it worked out that we could take a little trip to celebrate my graduation."

"See," said Claire with a sly smile, nudging Jacob's arm. "She's had like five different jobs in the past two years." *I'm surprised she can even afford a vacation.*

"Is your dad going with you?" Said Josie.

"Yep. We're going to take him along with us." He said giving her a knowing look. "It'll be good for him to get out of the house."

"How wonderful," she replied.

"So how about you? What are you doing tonight?" Nick asked.

"I'm supposed to be going to a movie in Yankton with Kim, but..." she began, tucking her hair behind her ears.

"Oh, what movie?!" Allison interrupted, setting her bulging backpack on the asphalt ground.

"*Fire in the Sky.*" said Josie excitedly, a broad smile on her face. "I've been waiting for it to come to the theater so I can hardly wait to go! It's about this guy who was abducted by aliens..."

"Allegedly abducted." Interrupted Chris, looking very skeptical.

"Okay, whatever." Josie waved him off with her hand. "So he was allegedly abducted by aliens out in a forest then returned five days later. It's based on true events."

Nick laughed at Josie's excitement. "I've seen the trailers and think it sounds fascinating. You can tell me all about it next week when I'm back from vacation."

Josie looked admiringly at him. "Okay. I can do that. Just give me a call when you get back and we'll meet up." Claire could tell from the lingering looks on their faces that they really did like each other. Nick was a nice young man; tall and built like an athlete. He was intelligent and good looking, an Honor Student and a vital member of the basketball team. From what Josie had told her, Nick was involved in their church youth league and had even gone on a mission trip to Kenya the prior summer for a month.

Surprised he turned out so well, Claire thought, *considering he's got no father and his mother is a drunk.* She tried to recall the mother's name but couldn't place it right then. *I wonder if she's working now or got fired again, like her two prior jobs.*

"So you said Kim is going with you tonight?" asked Chris, bringing Claire's attention back to the group.

"Well, yea, she's supposed to pick me up at 5:30 but earlier today she said she wants to go to some party down by the river." said Josie.

"How dangerous. What if someone falls in?" Allison piped up.

"I heard of that party place. I've been down to that spot once, it's pretty shallow there and the bank is pretty flat. Good for a bonfire or camping and room enough to park a dozen cars or so on the trail." said Chris.

"Oh really, Chris?! Been partying down there lately?" Nick chided him.

Squaring back his shoulders Chris said, "No Nick, it just happens to be a really great fishing spot too."

"Yea, Nick, it's true." Josie said. "My mom and some friends of hers took me fishing there once when I was a kid, I don't remember it cuz I was too young, but I do know we caught a pretty big catfish. My mom's got a picture of us." Claire immediately thought of the photograph from when Josie was about four years old. She was holding a catfish that was nearly as big as she was, with her mom squatting down behind her, helping support the weight of the fish. They were both full of smiles; so proud of the catch.

Claire smiled, equally proud to have that happy moment recorded on film. Considering she didn't spend much time at home, any memories made with her daughter were precious.

"Well, there won't be any fishing going on down there tonight." Allison said. "Unless you count guys fishing for girls to hook up with." She rolled her eyes and shook her head in disapproval. The boys both laughed at the analogy and agreed.

"You're right, Allison. Unfortunately a lot of them think that way.

You shouldn't go down there Josie." said Nick, taking Josie by the hand to indicate his seriousness.

"Oh, believe me, I don't want to." she said, shaking her head vigorously. "I told Kim I'm not going there with her and she promised me she'd drop me off at home before she goes to the party."

Josie had confided in her mother about Kim, telling her that Kim came from a divorced family and lived with her mom full time in a rundown house on the east side of town. Her dad lived in Minneapolis, a four and a half hour drive away, so she didn't see him much. Kim had really struggled with accepting her parent's divorce the previous summer and Josie befriended her, offering her an outlet and source of encouragement. Kim didn't hold the same Christian values that Josie did, but Josie knew she was being a positive influence on her new friend and even got her to attend her church youth group with her on a few occasions, of which Claire had commended her.

Nick said, "Okay. Sounds like you've got it taken care of then. I hope you enjoy the movie Josie." He hugged Josie tightly and turned to go. "I gotta run guys. My mom's probably wondering where I'm at." He gave Josie a broad smile and salute before jogging off toward his house.

"Have fun!" Allison said.

"Safe travels, see ya man." said Chris.

"See you next week Nick." Josie smiled and waved.

"Yea, I better get going too, my mom's gonna want help setting up for my brother's birthday party." Allison said, picking a pebble out of her sandal before picking up her backpack. "Josie, let's touch base in a couple of days and hang out, okay?"

"Of course my friend. I'll give you a call. Have fun tonight!" Josie said as she winked at Allison.

Josie and Chris walked toward their cars. "Do you have plans for this evening Chris?" asked Josie.

"Nope." He stated. "Well, I take that back. I'm supposed to go to my dad's tonight with my brother, but I really don't want to, so we'll see. I might still head up there, maybe John and I will ride the four-wheeler a bit or something."

"I bet some fresh air and four-wheeling is just what you need after these past few whirlwind days." Josie encouraged him as she set her bag and purse into the back seat of her Impala. "Get a few laughs in with your brother; do a little male bonding out there on the farm."

"Yea, you're right. Throwing a little mud up with the four-wheeler would be fun right now. And I'm sure dad would appreciate it especially since he missed the graduation ceremony." said Chris.

"Oh, I'm sorry. I was so busy that afternoon that I didn't realize he wasn't there, Chris." Josie said as she came around the car and walked closer to him. "That must have been disappointing to you."

"Well, yea, a little but it's planting season so he's gotta get the crops in the fields. That's a little more important right now than seeing his kid walk across a stage wearing a robe just to get a little piece of paper. That wasn't even signed!" He laughed but Josie could see sadness in his eyes.

"Yea, I'm sure that's a lot of work, but not taking a few hours off from planting to see his eldest son graduate from high school must be a hard pill to swallow." Josie said, her eyes misting over. "I'm going to pray for you." Josie laid her hand on Chris's shoulder and began to pray.

"Lord, thank you for Chris, for his talents and the hard work he put into high school. Thank you for his friendship to so many, and encouragement to those in need. Grant him peace now and comfort him with your Spirit. We know that all things work together for those who love You, [1] and Chris does love You. We also know that You have a plan for each of us, a plan to prosper us and to give us hope. [2] Grant Chris hope now, and peace, as he deals with his dad and the divorce situation. Guide him in Your ways. We ask this in Jesus' name. Amen."

"Thanks Josie." Chris leaned in for a hug. "I appreciate that. You're a good friend and I'm gonna miss you."

"Me too." She smiled up at him, "But we'll stay in touch and when I'm back here to see my mom we can see each other too."

"Deal."

As Claire watched her daughter drive away, she felt a surge of pride well up at the knowledge that not only was Josie an excellent student, but well respected and loved by her friends and teachers. Never before had she witnessed that first-hand, but seeing the yearbook messages and hearing Josie speak to her friends with such grace, kindness and maturity left her speechless. For the first time in a very long time.

"I rarely got to her volleyball games or concerts on time so I didn't see her interact with others. And we already know how I was at church for pete's sake. So dumb." She avoided his gaze as tears welled up. "I just assumed she was a good kid cuz she never gave me any trouble and her grades were always good and it seemed she could talk to me easily. At least when I was home she did. I figured she talked to her friends more often. But to see it now. To hear her being so kind and humble..." Emotions choked her words as a long minute ticked by. "She really was wonderful despite my parenting."

She took Jacob's hand. "I'm envious, "she whispered.

CHAPTER 15

The In-between Place

Claire leaned against the tree stump while Jacob picked up his fishing pole and cast it into the clear water. Silver backed fish darted under the pristine ripples, back and forth, first in then out of the shadows as though playing tag.

Remorse hung heavy upon Claire's chest and she focused on the shiny river rocks resting at the bottom of the shallow river; just like them she was submerged and heavy. Neighbors and church people, Josie, herself. She was constantly letting people down. But she sure was good at judging others. Super good at being rude, arrogant and vain. *Have I ever been a good mother?*

Without skipping a beat Jacob spoke up from the river bank. "Remember that time you bought Josie a horse? Remember it's name was Ronald but it was a girl horse so you told Josie to change the name to something appropriate and she refused?" Jacob's laughter was bubbly and genuine as if seeing the moment play out before him.

He knows? Of course he knows. Claire couldn't help but laugh with him at the memory of "Ronnie" as she and Josie so lovingly called the old Palomino.

"Yes, what a rotten name for a female horse. But Josie just rolled with it. Even tied pink bows in its mane, saying that Ronnie would appreciate them." A photograph of that girl and her horse riding across the prairie of the Jim River bottom would always be Claire's favorite. It hung in her living room, a constant reminder of better days.

Glancing at Jacob she saw the face of her daughter reflected back. His dark hair and the way it naturally parted on the left side, the shape of his face and those green eyes. *Could he be...?*

"Or how about that food fight you had when you were making banana bread but you dropped the glass pan and it broke, so she threw the batter at you, then you threw flour at her..." he trailed off into a fit of giggles dropping his fishing pole and doubling over with laughter.

Claire laughed and rolled her eyes. "We were cleaning up that mess for a week! And I made us shake hands and swear to each other we'd never, ever in the history of ever, have another food fight again!" Her gut hurt from laughing so hard and she took a minute to recover. Wiping happy tears from her face this time, Claire knew she had, on many levels, been a good mother to Josie, fun even, but not consistently or even more often than not.

"So how do you know about that stuff anyway?" She asked when the laughter faded, curious at the boy's knowledge of events so long ago.

"Oh, God tells me or shows me things sometimes. Things that might help us talk."

Claire pondered that notion as she fingered a velvety green leaf on a nearby branch, careful not to pull it too hard lest she pluck it from its life source. *This literally feels like velvet. Amazing.*

"But seriously Claire, you're not a bad person. God created you and everything He made is good. You have a purpose and He has a plan for you." He reeled in his line only to cast it again. "You've made mistakes and Satan's going bring those mistakes to your mind to try to make you feel bad about a lot of stuff. He'll bring up the past over and over again trying to get you to live in defeat and regret, but you can fight against him with the help of the Holy Spirit." [1]

Claire took a deep breath and dug her toes into the sand, letting the coolness wash through her body. Laying back and relaxing under the shade, she let her mind drift off with the breeze and think about the things she'd seen with Jacob. Her attitude, she knew, was preventable. No matter what other people do or say, she knew she was still the only one responsible for her actions, reactions and words. It was easy to be rude and distant; hard, so hard, to be kind and loving and patient, especially when the hurdles of life come up unexpectedly. And often.

She knew she was capable of love and joy and compassion. She recalled the many hospital patients and family members who had approached her, or left a note upon being discharged, to the effect of how wonderful she had been with them. How accommodating and pleasing to talk to, and how her sense of humor, albeit sarcastic, made their hospital stay tolerable.

She had been commended previously for her bedside manner by her coworkers and superiors, but thinking now on how she treated her own daughter she wondered how sincere her actions were. When, behind closed doors, when her boss or co-workers weren't watching, she could be so heartless and snide.

Love was hard. Loving others through their own attitudes or misgivings, through their immature years and refusal to change, was so difficult. Keeping them at arm's length was easy. To keep herself hidden and living basically as a recluse was easier than being vulnerable and risking the possibility of falling in love again, of trusting anyone else again even if it was a neighbor or church friend, a confidant, with whom she could simply talk to to avoid the loneliness that plagued her.

Jacob's voice interrupted her thoughts. "You've been really sad and angry. For a lot of years you've been getting further and further away from God and that's making everything worse in your life. I just wanted to talk to you for a while, maybe show you some things that would help you understand what happened. Maybe then you can find God again."

Giving him a glare, she hissed. "What? Find God?"

She sat up completely, allowing the anger to overflow, very well aware that their shared laughter of a few minutes ago was long gone and forgotten. "I'm supposed to find God? He's the adoring shepherd and I'm the lost sheep, is that it?" She flung her arms in the air as she spoke. "So isn't the shepherd supposed to take care of the sheep? He's the Boss, right? The Great Almighty. The One in charge of everything. The One that keeps track of everyone. So why am I the one who needs to find God?" [2]

What does this child know about anything? She stood but didn't feel her fists clenched in rage until she noticed Jacob staring at them for longer than necessary. Her breaths were fast and shallow and she could feel the ache forming in her temples and clenched jaw line.

"Maybe He's the one that's abandoned me." She seethed through clenched teeth. "I've been going to church and Bible study and... and...

giving of my time and... my money and for what? I'm alone and miserable and some days borderline psychotic I swear." She turned in an exasperated circle before flopping herself to the ground in a huff. "I work my tail off and get nowhere in life. I never take vacations cuz I have no one to go with. My family abandoned me, my husband died and I don't speak to my daughter. So forgive me for being a bit cynical toward God, but it doesn't seem that He's been doing me any favors lately." She finally stopped to take a ragged breath.

"He died for you." [3]

Claire winced at the sting of his words and dropped her head into her hands, check mated by his blunt honesty and shaken to the core for her doubt of God's role in her life. She'd been raised Catholic by a family, and a church, steeped in the tradition of the Biblical stories of Jesus' birth, teachings and death for all sinners. She knew in her mind that God made the ultimate sacrifice by sending his son Jesus to die as an intercessory scapegoat for all mankind, but seemed to, throughout the years, forget how big of a price that was for one man to pay for all mankind's wrongful ways.

Another thin layer of hardness fell away from Claire's heart as the boy's words sunk in. A gentle reminder that the sacrificial significance of God's Son doesn't change because of man's lack of reception or appreciation of it.

Silence rose between them as the birds chirped and the breeze danced with the tall brome grass, swirling it first this way, then that, like synchronized ballerinas.

"Yes. I know that." She said softly, her pride trampled and anger abated for the moment.

"And He offers us eternal life and gives us joy and peace through the Holy Spirit." [4, 5]

Claire nodded in agreement, "Uh huh." *That's how it was supposed to work*, although she hadn't known peace or joy for many long years.

"And if we confess our sins to God and ask for His forgiveness when we do bad things, then we can..."

"Hey, if you're referring to what happened with Josie, then you can just stop right there." Claire felt her pulse quicken as she scolded the child with her index finger. *So much for self-control.* Satan certainly knew her triggers, and her weakness for giving into her vices, and so she continued.

"She lied to me. She snuck around behind my back and lied to me about a *lot* of things mister and I will *not* take that from any child of mine. She was raised to do the right thing and she completely went against that." Claire stood again, fists clenched by her sides, lips trembling. "I didn't have a choice in the matter. What happened was a terrible problem and I fixed it. I took care of her. She's my daughter. It's my job to take care of her and do what's best for her no matter what."

Keenly aware of the silence around her, she blinked away tears and tried to focus on the boy. He stood with his eyes closed, face and palms raised to the warm sky. After several minutes he tilted his head to the side, looking at her with the kindest eyes she'd ever known.

"There's more you need to see." He said softly, taking her hand.

CHAPTER 16

The James River bank – late May 1993

Country music, too loud for comfort, blared from the local radio station and young voices rose merrily into the night sky all around Claire. A heavy weight fell onto her shoulders as she opened her eyes and found herself in her already assumed location. The middle of a party. *That* party. The one Josie was adamant she did not want to attend with Kim out of wariness at the potential danger - physically and morally. Looking around her, Claire could see why.

Claire started to turn away, scared of what she might see and worried it might be the truth. "It's alright." Jacob said, putting his arm around her waist, keeping her in place. "God is always with you. His strength will help you understand why things happened like they did."

With reluctance Claire made her body adhere to her mind's request to look around.

There appeared to be at least sixty teenagers scattered along a hundred foot section of the James River bank which was cleared of branches and trees and level enough for lawn chairs and tents. An ideal camping or fishing location with its seclusion from the gravel road and neighboring farms; bordered by the river on one side and thick tree grove on the other with just a narrow foot path to serve as the entrance.

Fallen trees and piles of branches edged the clearing; pushed aside by those who chose to make this spot a permanent gathering place. A careful chainsaw wielding individual must have, at some point, cut up multiple logs to serve as seating, au-natural, inside the space with the remaining collection of logs cut into smaller pieces and set aside to be used in bonfires. The large stack was carefully arranged, pyramid style, on top of wood pallets and covered by a tarp to protect it from the weather.

A teepee shaped bonfire, nearly six feet tall, loaded with thinner branches and larger chunks of wood, burned intensely in the center of the clearing. Its flames licking the darkening sky. Some kids gathered around it despite the summer heat, others were in lawn chairs, sitting on stumps of trees or hanging out in small groups laughing at private jokes and sneaking glances at members of the opposite sex.

A fifty gallon barrel was positioned on the far side of the clearing from Claire for those people who actually cared to discard their trash properly. As she was contemplating how much of a mess this many teenagers could make, someone across the clearing yelled "Incoming!" and threw a glass beer bottle at the barrel. It crashed with a resounding *bang* and shattered inside the container. Those who were closest to the barrel whooped and hollered, admiring the boy's aim; his buddies giving high-fives for his accomplishment.

Claire noticed probably half of the teens were holding either a can or bottle of beer, while most of the others had plastic cups full of another liquid. As she looked around she noticed a small, perhaps four-person tent, set up on the north edge of the clearing just inside the wooded area, and another slightly larger one behind it. The smaller one was on the edge of the campfire light but the second larger one was hidden in its shadows, unnoticeable unless you were on the far side of the smaller one. The zippered front of the smaller tent was open and two girls and a boy went inside for a minute, empty handed, then emerged with liquid filled plastic cups in hand. *A booze tent. Clever to keep that hidden, I guess.* Not that it would have mattered either way out here a half dozen miles from town, in the river valley, a quarter mile from the gravel road. This spot was well hidden from the road and only if you knew which trail off the gravel road to take would you be able to find the location.

"....*she ain't a Cadillac and she ain't a Rolls, but there ain't nothin' wrong with the radio...*" The country music was reverberating through the trees and across the river; the half moon a witness to the fiasco. Several of the teen girls were shaking their chests and swaying their hips as they danced flirtatiously in the clearing. Tight fitting tank tops paired with cutoff jean shorts were most females' choice of attire, and they were entertaining the majority of the teen boys, seen looking the girls up and down with what Claire would describe as "lustful eyes". *How disgraceful.*

A large group of kids were clinking their drinks together for toast after toast to "the good life!"; "the end of that damned high school!"; "to a hot, wet summer!". "Live free in '93!" one boy shouted above the rest to the cheering approval of the group. Glasses and bottles were raised to salute the toast and Claire realized they were many of Josie's classmates, the newly graduated seniors. Jolene, Kevin, Ray, Connie, Kristi, Andrea, Tom and Scott... several recognizable faces from her daughter's various activities in school. It shocked her to see some of the kids at such a party as she knew their parents as upstanding, church-going folks. Well respected in the small town. *This is unacceptable! Certainly they wouldn't approve of such crude behavior.*

Two boys were sitting on lawn chairs with fishing poles in hand, appearing to be actively trying to fish. With all the noise around she thought they'd be lucky to catch anything but then Claire saw the one boy reel in a decent sized catfish and she admired them for their efforts, despite the case of beer that was sitting between the two chairs. Not nearly old enough to drink, Claire guessed the attendees to be mostly juniors and seniors from East Valley School, with a few exceptions such as Kenny, a local farm kid who quit going to school after his Sophomore grade year so he could get more involved with their family farming operation.

Claire knew the family well as they just lived a few miles apart from one another, she in the river valley and they in the uplands, just north of Claire's acreage. Then there was a load of boys from a nearby town who had recently shown up. She and Jacob watched them walk into the bonfire light with their own beers in hand. *Already drinking and driving. Wonderful.* She overheard some of the girls talking about how cute they were and "who invited them?!"

"Oh my god! I'm so glad you're here!" A shorts and halter top wearing girl squealed as she pushed her way past her friends and ran across the clearing flinging herself into one of the boys' arms, forcing him to either grab onto her butt and hold her up, or drop her. He didn't disappoint, but instead held her close and began kissing her aggressively.

His friends turned away from the couple to check out the other girls, of which several came sauntering toward them, drinks in hand and 'come and get me' smiles on their faces. "I think the tent's free." The kissing girl stopped long enough to tell her plaid shirt clad mate, hopping out of his arms and leading him by the hand to the larger tent. *A make-out tent? Sex tent more likely. Oh geez...*

Just then a commotion started near the river where the boys had been fishing. A loud splash and high-pitched yelp from a female. Instantly Claire thought someone had fallen into the river. After a few moments, some gasps and a "what the hell is that?" comment could be heard as one of the fishermen dragged an animal up the bank and toward the fire. Claire craned her neck to get a better look at what was happening. The boys had caught a rather large snapping turtle and were dragging it by the tail toward the fire. Several other boys jumped at the chance to taunt and beat the animal with sticks that had been heated in the flames, leaving burn marks on the shell and stabbing at its head and limbs. The turtle tried to retreat into its shell but to no avail. The torture devices found their way inside the shell and pretty soon it was evident that the turtle would not be surviving this attack. Claire felt nauseous watching such demoralizing and wretched behavior and told Jacob she wanted to leave. Just as she turned she saw the boys fling the turtle into the bonfire.

More laughing and congratulatory remarks to the torturers echoed in her ears. Claire nearly vomited watching the events unfold before her. She closed her eyes but still couldn't block out the cheers and defamatory remarks coming from the teens' mouths.

"Well, this is about as stupid a thing as I've ever seen." She turned away from the disgraceful scene before her and led Jacob quickly through the trees along the tramped down grass trail that led away from the river. There were more than twenty cars and pickups parked haphazardly along the edge of the tree grove, on the grass trail and into the adjacent field, their awkward parking angles further evidence of irresponsible, teenage drivers. Vehicles jetted out into a row-crop field, squashing the newly emerging plants and ripping up the fresh earth with deep tire tracks. Claire fumed at the teens' nonchalant disrespect to the land owner. *These kids are so dumb. Why don't their parents raise them better? Give them some manners and a reason to use them. Holy crap!*

One of the pickups parked next to the tree line was still running with its driver's door propped open allowing the music she'd been hearing to escape and filter its way through the trees to the clearing. *Kudos to them. I'm impressed they're smart enough to leave the pickup running, instead of depleting the battery.*

Jacob caught her hand as she stomped toward the gravel road. "We're not leaving yet. Josie's just getting here." He said as a set of headlights came over the slight rise of the hill and toward them.

"So she did come here. I knew she was lying to me." she said, a slightly satisfied smile crossing her face. Sadly, knowing she was right didn't make her feel any better.

CHAPTER 17

"It's just for a few minutes!" The driver yelled as they emerged from the car. Claire recognized the driver as Kim, Josie's classmate and supposed friend, dressed now in denim shorts and a thin tank top. "Chill out!" Kim slammed the door and started to walk toward the party. Josie jumped out of the passenger side and ran after her, catching up just a dozen feet from where Jacob and Claire stood.

Breathless, with hair flying wildly with her movements, Josie grabbed Kim's arm and turned her around, "I don't want to be here. I already told you that. Just take me home." Her daughter's angry, persistent tone of voice startled Claire. She'd never heard Josie speak like that to anyone.

Kim jerked her arm away from Josie, "I just need a few minutes to see if Dillon is here. If he's not, then I'll take you home, but if he's here then I'm staying." She said matter of factly, continuing to walk away.

Josie's exasperation was evident as her voice rose an octave and she rushed forward, planting herself in front of Kim, blocking her escape path and forcing a confrontation. "You promised me you'd take me home before you came here, Kim."

"Oh my god." she rolled her eyes. "You're such a goody-two-shoes Josie. All your Jesus freak, church going days have made you incredibly boring. Have some fun for once in your life! Live a little, geez. It's not gonna kill you to go to *one* party."

Something behind Kim caught Josie's attention. Claire and Jacob turned to look, along with the two girls. It was another vehicle coming down the narrow grass trail. The excitement returned to Kim's angry face. "That might be them. Let's just wait here and see." They stood in the thick darkness of the night, only visible in the pickup's headlights. Kim smiled expectantly at the invisible occupants and Josie scowled as she looked at the ground to avoid being blinded by the lights.

As the pickup screeched to a halt, Josie could see cigarette smoke drifting upward toward the black sky and the driver tipped back a flask, its silver metal glinting a faint reflection of the dashboard lights. The driver, ignorant of how close he'd parked to Kim's car, banged his door loudly against her passenger side door as he jumped to the ground. Josie gasped and Kim laughed.

"Daddy will pay for that darling," the driver drawled, his southern accent the fakest one Claire had ever heard. He was fair haired and handsome; over six feet tall and muscular. An athlete's body clad in blue jeans, cowboy boots and a too tight plain white t-shirt. His distressed red baseball cap turned backwards.

"Dillon!" Kim actually jumped up and down a couple of times in excitement before leaping across the trail and grabbing the face of the driver, pulling him down to her for a deep kiss. Josie looked surprised as if Kim hadn't told her she and Dillon were that serious as to condone public displays of affection such as these. She looked away in embarrassment as Dillon grabbed Kim's butt with one hand and her breast with the other, pulling her erotically close to his body. She heard Kim moan with pleasure.

"Get a room." The occupant of the pickup chided, tossing an empty beer can into the bed of the pickup with one hand and opening another one with the other as he came around the tailgate. A bit taller than the driver and built with the same athletic frame. He was also fair-haired and handsome with country-boy clothes on like his companion except his baseball cap advertised a well known bank name rather than the other boy's "beer me" cap. The small detail made him seem more mature and he held out his hand to Josie. "I'm Boomer, this dipshit's cousin." He nodded to the kissing duo.

"That's a dumb name," Claire said. Jacob nudged her with his elbow. "Well, it is."

Taken aback, Josie looked baffled at the young man's odd name as well, and could only nod her head as she shook his hand. She still looked uncomfortable from the sexual display going on before her despite the darkness of the night.

"Josie." She squeaked. Boomer smiled broadly at her, looking her body up and down when Josie broke eye contact and turned away from him. The look did not escape Claire's attention and she felt her own body tense at the forwardness of the young man.

"Kim." Josie attempted to get the attention of her friend by grabbing her by the arm again, "Kim! I need to get home *now*." Kim untangled one of her arms just enough to shake Josie's hand off, then brought it back to Dillon, this time under his shirt sleeve, grabbing at his rather large biceps. "Kim, come on." She hissed through clenched teeth. "You promised me you'd take me home."

Kim came up for breath, not taking her lustful eyes off Dillon. "Sorry girl. No can do. My man's here now and we got business to talk about." She giggled at the innuendo as Dillon set her down on her feet, legs shaky with passion she wobbled and leaned her body against him.

Josie wedged herself between the two lovers and got in Kim's face. "I don't want to be here, please take me home. It's just a few miles, you'll be back in five minutes."

Kim clung to Dillon's arm for support and pushed Josie back with a hand to her chest. "Just chill out Josie. Holy shit. For once in your life just relax and have a good time." She turned to Dillon and grabbed his crotch, massaging a bit as she nuzzled his neck. "Babe, let's get outta here. I can't wait any longer." Dillon groaned with anticipation and slapped her on the butt, pushing her toward her car.

"Get in the back seat."

"Kim! Come on. Don't do this to me!" Josie's voice was getting more shrill by the moment as panic set in. But Kim wasn't listening. Claire's anger rose as she thought of what she'd do to Kim the next time she saw her. *That little bitch! How dare she treat Josie that way after all Josie did to befriend her.*

Dillon kicked his boots off on the grass and pulled his t-shirt over his head, the baseball cap falling to the ground with it. He called over his shoulder, "Gotta bail man! Plenty of ass up at that party. I"ll catch ya later!" His zipper was down next as Josie covered her eyes and spun around, nearly knocking Boomer over. She started walking quickly toward the gravel road, fists clenched in anger.

Claire's heart was breaking for her daughter, not only being left at this wretched party alone with no way home, but now discovering that her friend actually couldn't be trusted, and really wasn't a friend after all. She could sense Josie's sadness and see the anger in her body language knowing she had put her faith in someone who just betrayed her. *I know that feeling well honey.*

Josie hadn't gotten but thirty feet when Claire heard another empty beer can land in the back of the pickup, the swish of tall grass indicating that Boomer was walking behind her daughter, quickly gaining on her.

"Hey, wait!" he said to Josie's back. She didn't.

"Stop." He grabbed for her hand and spun her around, a bit too hard given her small stature as compared to his large frame. "I'll take you home. Get in the pickup."

She tried to take her hand back from him. "No thank you. I can walk. It's only a few miles." He wouldn't release her hand and stepped closer to her, completely blocking out what little light the bonfire cast upon her face.

"Just forget about those two horny-toads. Let's just get in the pickup and I'll get you outta here." With his free hand he pushed a loose strand of hair behind her ear, smiling broadly.

Sweat began to form on Josie's forehead. Claire could see her daughter's pulse quicken by the veins in her neck and assumed her mind was racing with escape options, just as hers was. The man's grip upon her hand looked tight and Claire knew Josie, the exceptional athlete that she was, wouldn't be able to outrun or out wrestle him. Her only hope was to get to the gravel road, a good quarter mile away, and across the barbed wire fence on the other side, then she could hide in the trees and gullies and make her way home through the pastures.

Once again Josie tried to jerk her hand away. "Thanks but I'm fine. I know my way in the dark." That comment made him laugh out loud as he released her hand and wrapped her torso with both arms, trapping her arms against her body.

"What else are you good at in the dark?" He sneered, flashing an evil smile as he smashed his lips upon hers, forcing her mouth open with his tongue. She squirmed but he was too strong. Before she could think or try and kick him, he spun her around clamping one large hand over her mouth and picking her up with the other arm around her arms and waist. "You're not leaving just yet girl." He growled into her hair. Her back was pinned against his chest, her feet a good five inches off the ground as he carried her toward the thicket of trees. Kicking was her only option but her heels were met with muscular shins, rock solid from lifting weights. Her eyes were wild with fear, nostrils flaring with breaths that came much too quickly and shallow.

Despite the weight of her body, Boomer easily managed to maneuver his way into the trees a few dozen feet, stepping over fallen trees and around samplings, where they were completely hidden from the outside world. Not that anyone would be looking for them anyway. Dillon and Kim wouldn't be coming out of their love nest for quite some time, and no one else knew they were at the party.

"NO!" Claire yelled and started after them. She wanted to intervene with Josie's attack, but found it impossible to move at the moment. It wasn't fear that stopped her, but an unseen force restricting her leg movements.

"Stop!" She yelled as she struggled against the force, waving her arms in the air but failing to get the attention of the boy or Josie.

"You can't get involved or stop it Claire. It's already done." She looked down at Jacob with huge fear-filled eyes.

"There's nothing we can do to change what happened and God won't let you see what that guy did to her. It's too painful and He's protecting you from seeing that." Jacob said sympathetically as Claire's body began to rock with sobs. She dropped to her knees, holding her head in her hands trying to stop the images that were going through her mind at what that bastard was doing to her innocent daughter.

She let out a gasp as though someone had gut-punched her when she heard Josie's muffled screams from the dark tree grove. "No, no, no, no, no..." was Claire's desperate plea as her fingers grasped her hair and pulled as if attempting to physically remove the thoughts from her mind's eye.

More angry than she'd ever been in her life, Claire waited. Gone were the crickets and frogs with their harmonious strains and rhythmic beats; silence now took center stage. Her thoughts were plentiful, wondering if she hadn't been working that night would Josie have been okay? Perhaps Claire's presence at home would have been enough for Kim to obey the instructions to drop Josie off at home after the movie.

The snap of a branch brought Claire back to reality a few minutes later as Boomer came out of the woods, twigs snapping under his heavy steps. He adjusted himself and a satisfied smirk spread wide across his face as he ran his hands through his hair. His long strides headed him toward the bonfire light and dozens of unsuspecting females.

Then mobility was Claire's again and she stood quickly, stumbling through the brome grass, and made her way into the trees where the boy had exited. The canopy of branches and leaves shut out any moonlight that even dared try to advance into the darkness, decreasing her visibility to nearly nothing so she followed the sound of Josie's sobs through the darkness.

Josie was standing on shaky legs, propping herself up against a sturdy tree as she pulled the hem of her navy blue sundress back down to her knees and adjusted the bodice, brushing the dirt and dried leaves off the large flowered pattern as she went. It was the same sundress Josie had worn to her high school graduation ceremony just a couple days prior. A crumpled article of light colored fabric lay nearby, bright against the dark earth and leaves and Josie stooped to pick it up, removing a twig and dried leaf from the folds. Claire didn't realize it was Josie's underwear until Josie reached up her skirt and used it to wipe off the blood on her inner thighs. Josie broke out into a fresh wave of sobs as she did so, looking embarrassed at the indecency of her situation and despite the darkness, she glanced around to make sure no one was watching her.

There was a fallen tree nearby and Josie kicked some dirt and leaves away from it with her foot and put the bloodied underwear on the ground, covering them up with the debris and leaving them unseen. "Jesus… I… need you," she uttered between sobs as she made her way out of the woods, the trees serving as leaning posts to steady her shaky legs.

Wiping unceasing tears from her face left smudges on Josie's cheeks, making them match the front of her sundress where she'd been forced onto the ground. Green eyes full of pain told a story no words could ever say.

Claire wanted so badly to help her but in this situation she could only witness and stare in disbelief. Josie had told her the truth and she hadn't believed her. *All these years, I was wrong. Josie had been innocent and was taken complete advantage of by that bastard.* There had been no inappropriate behavior or flirting between them. Josie hadn't been secretly buying or wearing scandalous clothing, or lying about where she'd been and certainly hadn't lied about being involved with other boys up until now. Claire's breath caught in her throat. Her heart stopped; her eyes dropped shut involuntarily.

If she thought her guilt was bad before, it was immeasurable now. Her heart broke a little more with every shaky step Josie took out of the dark woods, the snapping of each branch adding to the weight Claire felt on her shoulders. She dropped to her knees. Shame and overwhelming sadness overtook her and she sobbed, the pain emitting from her lungs as painful groans and screams of agony as Josie walked into the darkness alone.

CHAPTER 18

The In-between Place

"She walked home from the river?" Claire exclaimed, surprised at the fortitude of her daughter after such a horrific event. "Nearly three miles?" Exhausted, her tears spent, she brought her head up out of her hands and opened her eyes. They were back on the green banks of the river and Claire felt so relieved to be out of the darkness and somewhere safe.

"Yes." said Jacob, the breeze picking at his hair.

Claire stared at him in horror. "And the next day. I... I remember that day." She was wide-eyed and visibly shaken. "I got home from work just after seven a.m. and she was sleeping. I went to bed and didn't get up until after three o'clock that afternoon. She was in her room and I knocked on the door. She told me she had a really bad sinus headache and was resting. She gets allergies sometimes, you know." Claire thoughtfully looked off into the distant river bottom hills and continued. "I went to get a few groceries so I could make a casserole quickly before I went to work again at seven p.m." Tears started flowing down her cheeks. "I didn't even see her face to face that day."

She turned her tearful gaze back to Jacob, her voice turning a high pitch as her emotions choked out her voice. "I didn't even bother to look at my child's face, I just hollered through her bedroom door that there was a casserole on the counter and that I was leaving for work." The guilt on her face chiseled deep wrinkles in her forehead.

Looking down in shame she covered her face with her hands and shook her head, "What is wrong with me? I'm her mother, I should have taken the time to open the door and make sure she was okay or ask if she needed sinus medicine or a glass of water. She shouldn't have been alone."

"God was with her," Jacob said, his voice soft. "He never left her. Not even for a second." [1]

Claire scoffed and whispered back. "Huh. Little consolation for me. I'm the one that failed her. So many times."

"He's never left you either, Claire. Not once. Not when you last saw your brothers or when Alan died. Not when you moved to South Dakota or when you're at your loneliest and especially when you were thinking about ending your own life."

Claire's look of shame at the recollection that she was in *that* place of desperation just hours ago, showed her true feelings.

"When you feel the breeze on your face, that's Him. When you wake up to the smell of lilacs or the birds singing or hear thunder rumbling above you, that's Him. When your heart is overwhelmed with gratitude for the ability to see or hear or walk, that's Him. *All* good things come from God, and there are good things everywhere."[2]

Claire nodded in agreement.

"There are lots of good things in you too."

"Oh, well. I'm not so sure about that." she said. Her voice still raspy with emotion.

"Don't be so hard on yourself. You're hurting and you're human. Humans have free will and they live as they want to. They are harsh and say things with nasty tones and they get impatient and unkind. They forget about who created them and what they were created for."

Claire turned her tear streaked face to the boy. "I know who created me."

"And what you were created *for*?"

"I, um… yea. I guess so. Um… I was created to know about and love Jesus and to be like him." *Admit it Claire. You have no idea what you're here for.*

"You're right. We are made in the image of God and should try hard to become like Jesus. To be patient and kind, love others, be generous and have faith. We should be self-controlled and slow to anger, be joyful and humble. But our most important job is to worship God."[3]

"I go to church. I worship him." Claire felt her defenses flare again and heard it in her own voice. *Geez woman, calm down. Not everyone is out to condemn you with every comment they make.*

She tried a new approach, closing her eyes and bowing her head momentarily. *Lord renew in me a right spirit. Help me let each situation be what it is, according to your will, and not what I expect it to be based on my own wants or desires.* She silently hoped her prayer was heard.

Jacob nodded. "Yep. Lots of people go to church and lots of people worship him. But there's more to worship than singing songs, going to church or praying to him. We worship Him by keeping our minds, our lives and hearts clear of anything that can tempt us or pull us away from God. We worship Him with how we treat other people, how patient we are, how generous we are with our time, talents and money. We worship Him by submitting our own wants or desires to His plan and letting Him lead us, every day." [4]

As Jacob spoke Claire kept a mental list of her failings in the areas he described. She had failed miserably with Josie, allowing pride to take hold of her heart and ultimately allowing herself to commit an evil act on her own offspring.

Daily she gave into the temptation to keep her life simple by keeping others at arm's length. To stay so busy she didn't have time to foster relationships. Getting close to anyone meant vulnerability and vulnerability meant they might find out her deepest secrets or figure out she was a shell of a woman. All godly and christian as viewed from the outside, but inside she was rotting; slowly disintegrating under the pressure of guilt and fear from a life of selfish choices.

"We were also created to be around other believers. To encourage one another and be friends with other christians so we can help each other." [5, 6, 7] Jacob took up his game of tossing rocks into the river while he spoke, his face showing peaceful joy in such a childish act.

Claire inwardly chastised herself again. Sure, she helped at church. All the time. She took care of planning Bible School every year and substitute taught for Sunday school when needed. When various committees needed assistance she volunteered to help with food preparation, serving, decorating, cleaning or organizing whatever needed organizing, be it the kitchen cupboards or a fundraiser for the youth group. But to say she had any close friends in their church...? She sighed heavily at the silent admission.

Claire's neighborhood, within a six mile radius from the country church, consisted of her church members, many of whom had stepped up when Claire and Josie first moved to the area. The pastor had known they were settling in the area because of Alan's death and had spread the word about their arrival and situation, asking parishioners, specifically Claire's nearest neighbors, to assist her and her daughter in any way possible, reaching out to them as good stewards of Christ.

And they had. They had come to help unload the moving truck. They brought meals the first two weeks after arrival to help Claire get into a routine and get to know the nearby small towns and their amenities. They offered play dates with Josie and their children. If snow blocked Claire's long driveway that first winter, neighbors came to push the snow away and clear a path so Claire could get to work. Fact being, one elderly neighbor still pushed the snow out of her driveway when they got more than a few inches at a time; more than her small gas powered snowblower could handle.

She gave back to the community through the church by getting involved. Sundays were usually free, so volunteering her time at church functions and activities seemed the natural and right thing to do as a thank-you for those members who had helped her so often.

But to have a true friendship with anyone at church or with her neighbors? She was embarrassed to admit she didn't take the time to do that despite the efforts of dozens to try and befriend her. Mothers of children of Josie's age tried to get to know her but Claire kept them at arm's length, speaking of superficial topics such as the weather or whatever church or school activity was next on the schedule. If questions about her past were asked she changed the subject or simply excused herself to the kitchen or bathroom or somewhere other than where she was in order to avoid answering anything too personal.

Claire told herself that it was too painful to discuss Alan or her childhood, but if she were honest with herself she knew it was for reasons much deeper. She was ashamed. Embarrassed. Angry. Resentful. In complete denial about what she had done to put herself into the situation she currently faced.

Being a single mother, and a widower, was not the plan she had for her life. No one wants to be rejected by their family for choices they made, intentional or not. No one wants to fall in love only to have it ripped away from them. No one wants to have a child only to come to blame it for 'tying them down' to responsible adulting when their true desires lay out in the world, traveling and discovering its adventures.

Claire tried to see the good in life, her job, her health, but oftentimes failed at that too. Pushing the blame to her parents or Josie for her failed accomplishments and lack of happiness.

"Are you okay?" Jacob asked.

Claire jumped at the sound of his voice, surfacing from her wallow into self-pity. She nodded, brushed the hair away from her face and turned to look at his innocent eyes.

"I help at the church," she began hesitantly. "Whenever I can volunteer and it fits into my work schedule, I help with whatever they need."

Jacob's look implored her to continue.

A pain shot through Claire's heart. *The Holy Spirit.* Like a dagger, prodding her to examine herself. "But... I don't do those things because I love God."

Oh this sucks. This hurts. She writhed inside, trying to escape the gnawing feeling at her heart. Convicted.

"I know I do those things to try and make myself feel better and look better to other people. As if helping and staying busy and volunteering will pay my dues so I can be considered a good Christian, I guess." She swiped at hot tears, ashamed of her behavior.

"I want people to notice that I look nice and notice all the things I do so they'll say nice things to me and about me. Even though I'm not really that good of a person and inside I'm a total train wreck, at least I can look and play the part of a put-together woman." She shook her head more in disgust at herself than relief at finally admitting it.

She let her gaze wander to the sky, its sparkling blue hues peeking through the clouds and velvety green leaves as they swayed in the gentle breeze. "I'm selfish. I'm angry. I'm lonely. I'm resentful. And I'm a hypocrite. And I've taken it out on Josie her whole life because if it weren't for her birth, I'd have been a college graduate and world traveler. I would have had it all."

Silence fell between them while Jacob closed his eyes in prayerful communion, before speaking to her.

"Confession is good. It cleanses the soul and opens up the doorway between us and God." He began. "Keep in mind, Claire, that we all sin. [8] We all fail and do or say things that are bad or hurtful to others. That's why we need Jesus so much. He bore our sins and shame for us so that we could be forgiven by God." [9]

"Oh, yea. I know that." she said quietly. "But some things are unforgivable."

Jacob squatted down and drew three crosses in the sandy riverbank with his finger. "Two criminals were crucified near Jesus that day." [10] He pointed to the two smaller crosses. "And after the soldiers had beaten up Jesus and hung Him on the cross, one of the criminals admitted that he deserved to die because of the crimes he'd committed, but admitted that Jesus had done nothing wrong and should not die. He believed in Jesus right then and there, and then asked for Jesus to remember him after he died." Jacob looked at Claire with tender eyes.

"And then Jesus said they'd be together in paradise that same day. So you see, if we have faith in who Jesus is, and have an honest heart, God can forgive all things Claire. No matter how bad it is. The man's crimes must have been pretty bad if they crucified him as punishment. But God knew his heart. He knows your heart too. He knows what you've been through, your motives and how sincere you are." [11]

Shoulders heavy, Claire stared at the three crosses, the look on her face semi-convinced of Jacob's scriptural recount.

"And what about David?" Jacob continued. "He was a great man, very loyal to God and one of the best kings ever. But he took another man's wife as his own, he lied, and then sent the husband of that lady to be killed in battle. He did some bad things that made God unhappy, but what David did right was confess it all to God. He humbled himself before God and admitted his sins. He sought God's mercy and God forgave him and still loved him so much that He used his family to eventually bring Jesus to us as a baby." 12 Jacob took Claire's hand in his and remained silent until she looked at him.

"God is a God of love, not hate. He's always ready to hear us when we pray and He promised never to leave us. He's always been with you. You see, He didn't go anywhere. You did."

A soft moan escaped Claire's lips as she thought about how much time she'd wasted being selfish and vain, and rude to those around her. How many friendships she'd pushed away because of her insistence on keeping her sordid past a secret. The many years of time spent looking the part and appearing to be a good Christian, but pushing aside what would feed her soul or bring her true joy and peace.

"You know, as a kid I had a little white pillow with red pom-pom trim on the edges, and it said 'Please be patient, God isn't finished with me yet.'" She looked longingly off in the distance, recalling how she kept that pillow on her bed all through adolescence. Leaving it behind, like so many other things, when her parents forced her out. "He's still got a lot of work to do with this old gal."

"There's room for improvement in everyone."

"So how did Josie turn out so good? I mean, she's still a really good person. Right?" She chastised herself, ashamed for not knowing how her now adult daughter was. Ignorance isn't bliss when it comes to your only blood relative living just a couple of hours away. And you, all prim and proper, doing everything you can to ignore them because of selfishness and pride. "Probably gets that from her dad. He and his parents were always so nice to everyone."

She wiped her face and took Jacob's hand when he held it out to her.

CHAPTER 19

Omaha, Nebraska – October 2003

Ominous gray clouds, puffy and angry, hung low overhead and the bustle of Omaha's Old Market district enveloped Jacob and Claire as they stood on the cobblestone street in front of a single blue door. There was no identification except for the street number "702" on the window pane in gold metallic stickers. To the left of the blue door was a restaurant with patrons sipping on wine and laughing silently through the large street-side window. To the right was a novelty shop, closed now for the evening but showing off its African tribal masks, hand-painted landscapes and gorgeous Persian rugs through the lead glass window.

A lone man wearing a bright green t-shirt played his saxophone on the corner nearest them, the instrument case open at his feet for willing donations from passersby. A family with young children stopped to hear the music man, their toddler dancing to the rhythmic sound as his mom snapped a photo of the young child's talent. Couples strolled hand in hand, window shopping. The burnt orange and yellow leaves fell around them, collecting like rival gangs in the gutters and dark corners. Thunder rumbled in the distance, causing many folks to look skyward as if estimating how much time they had to enjoy the Old Market ambiance before the storm broke through the skies above them.

Jacob opened the door and ushered Claire through it and up a narrow flight of stairs to another door, windowless and brown, labeled with a sign reading "Rape Victim Support Group", with a list of days and meeting times below it, taped directly to the door.

"Carla, it's great to see you back this week." Claire instantly recognized Josie's voice as the blue door opened below them, the crisp fall air leading them up the stairs like a ghostly tour guide.

"Hi Josie. Thanks." Glancing back down the flight of stairs, Claire saw Josie hold the door as a younger woman walked through, the young woman's short red-ish brown hair and wide-set eyes visible beneath her baseball cap. "It really helped last week to talk about stuff, so here I am." She shrugged her slender shoulders as they topped the stairs and entered the meeting room.

Claire stared at her daughter, trying to remember the last time she'd seen her smile like that, so full of life and purpose. *Probably on her high school graduation day. Suppose I would have seen her smile like that on her last day of school, had I not been working. Oh what I've all missed to chase an extra dollar. I should have adjusted my work schedule to a day shift. Then I would have been there, and at her volleyball games and concerts and...*

Jacob placed his hand on Claire's back, indicating for her to follow the two women into the room.

A large wooden table, big enough to seat more than a dozen people, took up the majority of the space with an antique buffet table on the far end offering bottled water, cookies and a large coffee pot, steam rolling out of the top, filling the room with its bold aroma. Several other women were there already and more voices could be heard coming up the stairs as well. The chairs were quickly taken by attendees; women of all ages greeted one another and chatted quietly.

Josie was dressed casually in jeans rolled up on the cuffs, a periwinkle blue sweat-shirt and flip-flops. Some things never change, Claire thought, recalling how much Josie loved wearing the flimsy shoes as a teen. All summer long that's all she wanted to wear outside, despite Claire warning her about the dangers of stepping on a sharp twig or, god-forbid, a stray nail. Today her dark hair was pulled back into a low loose ponytail, tendrils softening her beautiful face. *Wow. She's so pretty. My Josie. My sweet Josie. How I've missed you.*

The young woman stood and the attention of everyone in the room turned to her kind smile and confident hands holding a fresh cup of coffee.

"Mmmm...." She smelled the hot brew. "Thank goodness this is decaf or I'd be up half the night watching soap operas and eating bon-bons!" Her comments lightened the mood, putting everyone at ease.

"For those of you who are new to our group, welcome. We are truly honored to have you here. My name is Josie, and I am the lead counselor, although we do have Amber here tonight as well to assist if you need a prayer partner or a sounding board." She motioned to a kind faced, fifty-something year old woman sitting in the back of the room, near the window, who smiled and waved at the group.

"Regardless of your situation or how long it's been since your trauma occurred, there is healing to be had and you are always welcome here, whether it's for two months or two years." She set the coffee cup down in front of her. "We are a Christian counseling service and focus primarily on God's healing power, knowing that healing also comes through prayer and by talking with others who have similar experiences, as well as some diet and exercise changes that can drastically help your healing process. There is comfort in knowing that others understand the struggles and pain you are experiencing, and are willing to share what they've learned, to assist you, encourage you and listen to you while you're on your journey." Sitting down, she took a sip of coffee. "Per usual, I'm going to open the floor up to anyone who needs to vent or wants to share their progress. No obligations, of course, sometimes we just need to be silent and let the process of being seen do its healing work too, so don't feel bad if you don't say a single word tonight."

Over the next two hours Claire witnessed her daughter counsel the group of women and listen to their struggles about their own rapes, with all the grace and confidence of a true professional. Some women spoke of their rape by strangers, a couple by relatives when they were children, and one by her own husband while he was intoxicated. The women were at various stages of their experiences, from a young lady whose violation had just occurred a few weeks prior, to other women who had been coming to the support group for several years. Claire marveled at how openly they spoke of their pain, their embarrassment, their shame and anger, and what their experiences had done to their self-esteem. The women owned their pain, they didn't push it out or off themselves onto another; they didn't hide it or deny it.

She held even more adoration for her daughter, whose compassion was unmatched when speaking to these women, holding one while she sobbed and supporting another who, in anger, screamed into a pillow, her wounds still very fresh in her mind and heart. Then listened as Josie spoke of forgiveness and self love, encouraging the women to let God heal them from the inside out. They prayed together, each woman taking her turn at bending God's ear to her concerns and requests. Each woman took one more step, however small it was, toward healing.

Claire saw how brilliant her daughter was and how her own rape and subsequent experience had shaped her into this loving counselor Claire now saw before her. The compassion and patience that twelve years of healing had given Josie was evident in her actions and words. The way she kept her composure and optimism while counseling such deep pain was something that couldn't be taught in any college or university; it had to be learned through experience.

"Ladies, you are deeply loved by a God that is healing you and restoring to you what was lost and broken.[1] Be patient with Him, and yourself, while He works." Josie was telling the group, speaking slowly to ensure they knew the weight of her words. "What happened to you does not define you or limit what you will become. Focus on the good, the blessings, the healing, not on the past or the pain it holds." She walked around the table as she spoke, making eye contact with each woman and laying her hands on their shoulders. "It helps to talk about it, many times, because each time you tell your story or speak of your pain, it loses its power over you." She stopped at the head of the table, folding her hands, "I'm going to pray over you before you leave tonight."

Claire turned to Jacob, questioning, "How did this happen? I mean, she seems so peaceful and... and, not angry at all, just happy and, and good... " Her voice trailed off as she examined her own hostility and lack of healing despite the passing of years.

"I was hoping you'd ask me that." Jacob smiled, turned and led her down the stairs and out the blue door.

CHAPTER 20

Creighton University, Omaha, NE – December 1993

Christmas melodies on light jazz notes floated through the air from a clock radio, tucked against the wall in the far corner next to a bookshelf lined with dog eared novels and outdated magazines. White twinkling lights and red ornaments adorned an eight foot tall Christmas tree that, including its base and top star, touched the high popcorn ceiling. Wrapped around the tree were strands of actual popcorn and cranberries that Claire recalled Josie telling her about on the phone that first winter Josie was in the dorms. The entire floor of girls in Jasper Hall had gotten together one evening in the commons area to string the goodies with needle and thread and Josie had recounted how many of the girls had poked their fingers with the needles, having not been accustomed to the task of sewing. The group of thirty-six girls had gone through an entire box of bandaids during the crafting session and Josie was proud that she did not use even one of them.

Josie had taken Home Economics her Sophomore and Junior years of high school, learning such things as how to string and use a sewing machine, read a sewing pattern well enough to make clothing by hand, bake bread from scratch, read ingredient labels and recipes, budget finances and other such skills a homemaker would need. Not that Josie's plans included being a full time homemaker, but the alternative class offered during that time was Agricultural Science - which absolutely did not appeal to Josie. Although several girls in her class did enroll and learned about animal anatomy, acres, bushels and yields, soil quality and other such farm related topics.

Josie and her boyfriend, Nick, were the only students in the lounge this Christmas Eve. Claire knew from Josie's college orientation packet that staying on campus during holidays was an option for students who lived out of state, had no family or money to travel home for the holidays. The cafeteria wasn't open during the holidays but there were plenty of grocery stores, restaurants and fast food joints within walking distance of campus that they could easily survive the breaks. And now, Chinese takeout containers littered the coffee table in front of the pair as they sat on the couch talking quietly and sipping hot chocolate.

"You should open your fortune cookie," Nick said, "Maybe it'll give you the winning lottery numbers." He chuckled and tossed the cookie into her lap.

Claire noticed that Josie looked sullen this evening; lonely despite Nick's company. He'd known Josie since the first grade. It hadn't taken the pair but a few days to befriend each other to the point that they were nearly inseparable. It helped that they rode the same school bus. They'd sit together on the bumpy bus rides to and from school, chatting about silly stuff, sharing their after school snacks on the hour ride to their respective homes, polishing off an entire pack of bubble gum, their mouths so full they could hardly breath. And god forbid they'd start laughing... which they did so often that they had to spit their huge wads of gum out before one of them choked.

Josie had shared those fun memories with Claire when she was younger and chatted non-stop about her life and friends, going into great detail about each one's personality and quirks to the point that Claire thought she was either going to become their best friend too or lose her mind from the incessant talking. Whichever came first. Looking back on those conversations now, Claire wished they'd never stopped.

As their senior year in high school arrived, Josie confided to Claire that she and Nick had started planning their future. They had declared their love for each other and had officially considered themselves a couple since the end of their Sophomore year, and best friends they certainly were, so the thought of going to separate colleges and not seeing each other save for a time or two a year when they might both be visiting their hometown at the same time, wasn't something either of them could fathom.

So they started looking at colleges that offered both of their respective majors, and planned to attend together. After months of research they'd finally settled on University of Pennsylvania in Philadelphia, nearly 1400 miles from small-town South Dakota. At first Josie had worried about the distance; she and her mother discussed not having the extra funds to fly her home for holidays but agreed that Josie could work on campus, through the Work Study Program offered to students. They were given x-amount of hours a week to help in the Admissions, Alumni or Registrar's Offices, and the boys were mostly assigned to Groundskeeping, assisting with mowing, pruning hedges and shoveling snow, which Nick planned to participate in as well, stating all his extra money would go to Josie to help her pay for visits home to her mom.

After that fateful graduation night, everything changed.

Josie had suddenly changed her mind and convinced Nick they should go to Creighton University in Omaha, Nebraska. Just a short two-and-a-half hour drive from their respective homes, Nick and Josie would easily be able to come back for holidays, or even weekends. Yet here they sat, that first Christmas holiday, alone in the dorms.

"I had to work that Christmas," Claire said. "Four days in a row to cover for a sick co-worker so Josie chose to stay at college. We actually spoke on the phone about it and she assured me Nick would be with her, so I'm glad to see them there together. It looks rather cozy and romantic." *I don't even know what that's like.* Thinking about her and Alan's early relationship, then a baby, then single motherhood. *No cozy romance in any of that.* She found herself fending off feelings of envy once again.

"You have to read it out-loud," he continued, nudging her with his elbow and smiling mischievously. His handsome face lit up the room as much as the tree lights did and Claire admired his handsome features..

Rolling her eyes, Josie said, "You're silly." She looked at the small white piece of paper and read it to herself then her smile faded and tears silently welled up in her eyes, leaving Nick in total confusion.

"Hey, whoa." Setting his mug down he scooted closer to her on the couch and put his arm around her shoulders, snuggling her to his side.

"Was it that bad? You gonna get hit by a meteor or something?" Nick tried to lighten the mood.

"I'm so sorry," she sniffled and leaned forward, grabbing a tissue from the box on the coffee table. *Carol of the Bells* started on the radio, the peppy rendition belying the dark mood that just covered the room. She leaned into his chest and rested her head on his strength. "I think I need to tell you something."

In the dim glow of the Christmas lights, Claire and Jacob watched the two as Josie told of the rape and subsequent abortion. Nick's eyes closed, pushing tears out, but his arm never left Josie's shoulders. He remained as her silent support in this most difficult of admissions, handing her tissues and taking the wet ones back from her to dispose of in one of the empty takeout containers that was labeled "Sweet and Sour Chicken".

"It was horrible Nick." Josie said after she'd calmed herself and the sobs ceased. "I didn't have a choice in any of it. What that guy did to me and then what my mom made me do... it was all forced upon me as if I didn't matter at all." She looked up at him with red rimmed eyes and puffy cheeks. "Like I was invisible and just standing on the sidelines watching it all happen to me."

He pressed his lips to her forehead, eyes closed, praying or composing his emotions and thoughts. Claire felt the need to sit down on the floor as the memories of those weeks took her stability. She wanted desperately to hug her daughter as Nick did now, to feel the closeness they once had.

Taking a ragged breath, he spoke. His voice was thick with emotion. "The fact that anyone laid an unkind hand upon you makes my blood boil, but I know what the Bible said about such things. *Be angry but do not sin*, and *vengeance is mine, says the Lord*.[1] That guy will pay the price for his sins. The Lord will not let him off the hook."

Nick rested his chin on the top of Josie's head and pulled her close as he thought through his next words carefully. "It's tragic and terrible that you had to go through that, Honey," he said gruffly, offering her yet another tissue then taking one for himself as he finally wiped his own tears, "I love you with all of my heart. For always. Nothing changes that. Not ever." He paused to take her face in his hand, looking her in the eye. "*Nothing* changes my love for you. Do you hear me?" She nodded her head.

"I'm sorry I couldn't be there for you after it happened." he said softly, emotion closing off his throat.

"You're here now."

Nick looked thoughtful for another moment before continuing. Leaning closer, Claire hung on every word he said; anxious to hear how he found understanding in Josie's situation. "I remember how different you seemed after graduation. I mean, after that night, er, um, when I got back from vacation, ya know." Josie shook her head in understanding.

"You went from being so vibrant and positive, outgoing and always involved in whatever was going on at youth group or with our friends to being sad and distant. I mean, you hardly came out of your house all summer."

Josie rubbed her thumb across the top of his hand. "Yea. It was a rough few months. But you kept me going just by telling me that you were always there for me. That you were my biggest fan and that you supported me no matter what."

He lightly kissed her lips and hugged her around the shoulders in response.

"I know I ignored most of your calls and I was distant and I'm sorry for that."

"Yea, I was pretty worried that you didn't want to date me anymore." he laughed. "Could have just kicked me in the shin and told me to take a hike."

Josie's laughter was such a relief to Claire's ears that she started crying. "That's the laugh I remember. It's been so long since I heard it, Jacob." Claire said. "So long." She gazed longingly at her daughter. "I thought I had ruined her forever... but look."

Nick's concern was heartwarming, "But I figured you'd tell me what was going on when you were ready." He brushed the hair back from her face. "I wish I could climb inside your heart and mind and help you fight this darkness. But know that I'm here for you. I'll be your strength. Me and God. Okay?" He tipped her chin up to look in her eyes.

She nodded, as tears overtook her and she leaned into Nick's strong arms. "You know she didn't even want me," she whispered a few minutes later.

Claire winced in surprise at the admission and the sudden change of mood.

"Whoa honey. Hold up now. How do you know that?" He supported her weight with his strong arms as a shocked look passed over his face as well.

"How does she know that?" Claire asked Jacob, who didn't bother to acknowledge her except to direct her attention back to her daughter.

"When I was packing for college last summer and diggin' in the attic for suitcases, an envelope fell out of an old shoebox. I read just enough of it to discover it was a letter from my mom to my dad when he was in Vietnam." She took a deep ragged breath before continuing. "I read them all. The letters were from my parents to each other and..." her voice cracked. Nick handed her another tissue and squeezed her tight, planting another kiss on her forehead.

"Oh man Josie. That sucks." Nick said.

"You know what? I've got them in my room, you can read for yourself. I'll be right back." And with that she hopped up and ran down the hall to her dorm room, returning a minute later with a ragged shoebox. One that Claire recognized immediately.

Pulling an envelope out, Josie quickly glanced at the contents then handed it to Nick.

"Start with this one."

Nick didn't look pleased to be reading someone's private correspondence, but took the letter nonetheless, reading to himself for a minute before speaking out loud.

She's got colic and doesn't sleep more than an hour at a time at night. I'm exhausted and angry at her. I didn't sign up for this Alan! I don't want this kind of a baby. You're the one that wanted her so bad. You should be here, not in Vietnam. It's such a dumb war anyhow. Just quit the Navy and let's move back to Nebraska.

"See," Josie interrupted with irritation in her voice. "She wrote that to my father when he was
off at war! I mean, who does that? Add more stress to him when he's supposed to be concentrating on
staying alive?"

"Yea, I..." Nick stammered.

Oh my gosh. How stupid of me to do that to him when he was already so stressed. Then to say those things about Josie? Honestly Claire. She dropped her head into her hands as the guilt mounted on her shoulders.

"And this one. Look at this one." Josie said, handing him another letter.

He read aloud.

Mother and Father, I'll get right to the point and pray you read these words. My husband Alan was killed in the war last week. I know you're upset with me for marrying him and having the baby, but I'm in a desperate state. I'm wondering if you'd consider taking me in for a while, until I get on my feet again. I would give up our daughter for adoption so I could pursue college, like I originally planned. I just want to come back home and have things go back to the way they used to be. Please consider my request. Always yours, Claire

Claire hung her head low, cringing against the truth. And how true those feelings were back then, when she was still so young and dependent on others for support and guidance. *No way did I wanna face life as a single parent with a fussy toddler.* She recalled her desperation so well, even now.

"That letter was unopened when I found it and addressed to a house here in Omaha." She raised her eyebrows at Nick, her implications obvious.

"Wow." said Nick.

"But it says "return to sender" on the envelope so either my grandparents moved or refused it but regardless, they never knew about her request and probably didn't even know about me." She blew her nose into a tissue and took a long drink of hot chocolate to push the emotions out of her throat.

"I thought her and my relationship was bad before then, but after I read those things about my mom and how she felt about me and being a mom in general, I actually hated her Nick. I honestly never wanted to see her again, but I did wanna be near my dad's family because they are, literally, the only other family I have. And maybe, I guess, I thought I could try to find my mom's family too. If they're still here, ya know."

"Yea, of course. I think we should try to find them. I think that'd be good for you." He reached into the box and pulled out another letter that was partially torn then taped back together. It was addressed to a woman named Eleanor.

> *Dear Mother, I hope this finds you well. Have you received my previous letters? I've sent you three of them these past several months just to you, hoping to hear back from you. Has father forgiven me? Does he even let you see the mail? Perhaps you didn't see my letters because he's keeping them from you? I don't know how else to reach you. Your phone number no longer works.*

"Whoa." said Nick. "Would your grandpa really have kept your grandma from seeing the mail?"

"Well I don't know, Sherlock." Josie said sarcastically. "I never met the guy."

Nick chuckled and reached for her hand. "I'm sorry Josie. That was a dumb question. It just sounds like he wasn't real nice."

Josie shrugged and spoke softly. "Not everyone is nice. Not even to their own family."

Leaning back onto the couch she propped her feet up on the coffee table, pressing her fingers into her temples to alleviate the obvious tension building there.

"You know, this sounds like a really poorly written soap opera Hun." His comment made Josie chuckle. "One I don't wanna watch and wouldn't recommend to my friends." He patted her knee. "But I gotta say it. You know what I'm gonna say don't you?"

Josie shrugged.

"Remember our youth group discussion about God turning bad situations into something good?" [2]

She chuckled, remembering their youth group 'experiment' as it were about a year and a half ago where the group had brainstormed one evening about the worst things that had happened in Biblical times and how God had turned them around to be something good. Their list included Joseph's feud with his brothers, Mary's unplanned pregnancy, and many others. After being serious with the assignment for a half an hour, they turned their imaginations on and started coming up with semi realistic, and completely unrealistic, scenarios in modern times that maybe could happen.

"Yea, like if the sun quit shining, God could make it possible that crops would grow not by sunlight but by humans singing to them every day." She said, laughing at the prospect.

He made her look at him. "Yep. God always provides a way. He always has a purpose for everything we go through and sees the tears we cry." [3, 4] She nodded her head in agreement even as fresh tears ran down her face. "And He is always with us no matter what. His Word says He has a plan for us, plans to prosper us; to give us hope and a future. He knows our desires and our pain. In Second Kings it says "I have heard your prayers and seen your tears and I will heal you".[5]

Josie was in his arms now, tightly held as he spoke and she sobbed. "Heavenly Father, fill Josie with your Spirit of peace now in Jesus' name. Give her that peace that passes all understanding and lift her up, heal her heart and mind and body from the pain she's in. Thank you for never leaving her side, for putting us in each other's lives and for giving us your Son, who heals all wounds, seen and unseen. We know You have a plan for her pain, that You will redeem and restore her as You promised to do. Give her wisdom and revelation to Your will, that her life may glorify Your name and further Your kingdom. In Jesus' name we pray. Amen."

"Amen." Josie whispered, squeezing Nick's torso tightly once more before letting go to pick up the fortune and show it to him. "*The truth will set you free,*" it read. They exchanged a knowing look. "Seems God wanted me to finally tell you all this and reveal to me that you're part of my healing." She said softly, laying her head on his shoulder again. "Thank you for praying for me. I feel like a huge weight has been lifted. Like I have hope now."

"Sometimes we just need to tell someone else about our troubles and have more people praying for us. I always pray for you, but now I know what to specifically pray for."

After a sip of cocoa, he said, "Hey, have you seen a counselor? Or talked to a pastor about this stuff?"

Disappointment shifted across her face as she shook her head 'no'. "Just you." she admitted.

"Okay. That's okay." He brushed tear streaks off her face. "But I do think a Christian counselor who specializes in these situations would be really beneficial to you. And I'll go with you, every minute, if you want me to. We're in this together."

CHAPTER 21

"Wow." said Claire, rubbing her arms to ward off the chills she'd just gotten. "I can't believe Nick was so understanding about it all. So calm and loving. Not judgmental and bitter or blaming Josie for what happened."

"Is that what you were used to growing up?"

The look she gave him said it all. "That's a rhetorical question. Right?"

The look Jacob gave her said he wanted to hear more.

She shrugged, chuckling despite her apprehension of the subject. "Yep. That's my childhood summed up in one word. Judgmental. Felt it all the time from my dad; I was never good enough. None of us kids were. Didn't feel it so much from my mother. She may have been more reserved in her affections, you know, not the lovey-dovey, warm and fuzzy kind of mother, but she was understanding of the teenage girl drama I had at school for a while, and the acne I struggled with for a few years. And then when I grew three inches in one summer she took me shopping to buy clothes that fit so I wouldn't be embarrassed at school."

Claire smiled at the memory of their discrete talks when her father was at work or had disappeared into his office, scotch in hand. Her mother didn't usually say much, so when she did Claire made sure to listen.

Really, she was remarkable. How did she talk so easily to me when I can't even talk myself out of a bad mood?

"And she supported my dreams of leaving Omaha to pursue an architectural career in a far off city." Her eyes misted over thinking about the huge smile her mother revealed when Claire told her of her plans. "*That's a fantastic plan dear.*" Her mother had declared. "*A marvelous use of your talents and intelligence. I'm excited to see where your dreams take you.*"

I wonder what dreams she gave up to marry father and have a family. Why didn't I ever ask her?

"It sounds like she truly loved you. In her own quiet way." Jacob said.

Claire nodded. "Yea. She did. I know that. And I feel bad that I lied to her about various things but I think she had a lot on her plate dealing with three kids and my dad." She paused to unfold and refold the hem of her shorts, contemplating her next words.

"I wonder why she stayed with my father if she wasn't really happy with him."

Jacob was reflective for a moment before speaking. "Love is a choice. She chose your father in marriage and that means even when times were tough or his behavior wasn't kind, she chose to love him. Just like God chooses us. Even when our behavior isn't loving or respectful toward God, He still chooses to love us. So much that He sent His Son to die in our place. Sacrificial love in its purest form."

Claire's eyes misted over. *I feel like I sacrificed a lot for Josie. My sanity, my sleep, my love life.* She laughed out loud at her thoughts.

"Nick loves Josie." Jacob continued, as if knowing Claire's current thought pattern would lead her down a road of despair and regret. "His love and support of her come from a place of understanding God's use of trials and hardships to mold us into His masterpiece. Even if it's something as tragic as rape. You see, Josie wasn't to blame for what happened to her and Nick knew she needed his unconditional love, not anger, to help her through the situation."

Anger. Oh to be that understood. Claire's voice was soft. "I was surprised to see Josie wasn't super angry. I mean, given the situation and all."

"She was plenty angry, but she faced her problems right away. She didn't run from them."

There he goes again, pointing out my faults. Claire gave him a disapproving look. Her mouth tight.

"Yea, yea, point made Jacob. I get it. I'm a screw up."

"I'm not blaming. Just stating facts about Josie's healing journey. Come on."

CHAPTER 22

Omaha, NE – February 1994

In a well lit hallway with red painted doors jutting off to the left and the right is where Claire saw Josie this time. She was alone. Standing against the wall looking nervous in her white sneakers, blue jeans and pale yellow, two-sizes-too-big sweatshirt. She looked like a wreck, as if she hadn't slept in a few days. Hair disheveled and eyes puffy, she picked at her fingernails with her front teeth, a nervous habit she'd had since childhood when Claire thought she'd weaned Josie from sucking her fingers.

Several individuals came through the hallway, filing into one of the rooms just beyond where Josie stood. Claire walked past her daughter and read the sign on the door "Rape Victim's Support Group". Peering through the small pane of glass on the door, Claire was surprised to see that not just women were in attendance. Some men attended with what appeared to be wives or daughters, or perhaps just friends, and one man in his mid twenties sat alone. Several women were younger, about that man's age, but two others were older - perhaps in their forties if Claire had to guess. The attendees mingled, chatting quietly and sipping coffee obtained from a small table on the far side of the room.

"There you are." she heard Josie say. Turning to look back down the hallway again, Claire saw Nick rush through the front door and give Josie a tight hug.

"Had a flat tire on my bike," he said, winded, "Ryan loaned me his; once I tracked him down in Grafton Hall. He was playing Nintendo with Matt and Will."

"Go figure." She managed a small smile, relieved to see him.

"You ready for this?" putting his arm around her shoulders and pulling her close.

Josie nodded, keeping her arms crossed in front of her in protection of what appeared to be a fragile little girl.

Claire felt a stab of guilt pulse through her. *I did that to her. I took my strong beautiful daughter and made her frightened and weak. Does every mother feel this way when they realize they messed up their kids?* And this wasn't something small like telling them they probably shouldn't be playing basketball because they're only five foot tall and keep dribbling the ball off their feet. This was major damage. The kind that destroys young people and drives them to drugs, alcohol or suicide. Or any combination thereof.

The room was quite large with a dozen or so chairs placed around a rectangular table. Those in attendance were friendly enough to move a chair to the left, allowing Nick and Josie to sit beside one another, with the young single man offering to get them both coffee before taking his place at the table. After several people shared updates on their lives, their healing process and struggles of the past couple of weeks, the group leader asked Josie if she felt comfortable enough to share as well. Josie looked at Nick, worried lines creasing her forehead.

"It's okay. This is a safe place and I'm right here beside you." Nick said, his arm tightly around her shoulders.

Josie nodded, fidgeting with her fingers and the now empty coffee cup sitting before her. A woman from across the table slid a box of tissues to her. Josie chuckled and wiped tears away from her face, beginning her story with the classic words heard in that room, "My name is Josie. I was raped." She took a long ragged breath.

"It happened last May, at a high school party that I didn't want to be at, by a guy I didn't know." She looked at Nick through teary eyes. He gave her an encouraging smile and nodded for her to continue. The young woman went on to describe being carried into the woods and forced to the ground, on her stomach.

"I have scars on my arms from where the sticks cut my skin." she pointed to a faint white jagged line on her left arm, tracing its path with her finger. "I told my mom I tripped and fell outside, but I never told her the truth of what actually happened." Her look was distant. "Not until I realized I was pregnant."

Tear-filled eyes again searched for Nick's and held them for a moment while she gathered the courage to continue. Looking back down to her restless hands. "She forced me to have an abortion."

The women who had given Josie the tissues gasped a bit too loudly, quickly covering her mouth in embarrassment and turning her gaze downward to avoid eye contact with anyone. "I'm so sorry." she offered, shaking her head. Others mumbled their "I'm sorry", "You poor thing" and "That's terrible" comments as a show of support.

The woman next to Josie reached out to rub her on the shoulder and said, "I've been there too young lady." Which surprised Josie as the woman appeared to be in her 40's. "When I was thirty-four I was raped by a man who lived next door to me in a four-plex apartment building. One night he heard me opening my door with my keys, stepped into the hallway to say hello, then punched me so hard I lost consciousness. I got pregnant but miscarried a couple months later." Her eyes were large and brown, overflowing with tears that spilled onto her red blouse leaving small dark water marks like ladybug spots. "That was just over ten years ago and I'll tell you what honey, time does heal some things," she raised her eyebrows, "but other things God has to heal. There's just no other way to get it done." Her smile dominated her tear streaked cheeks as she squeezed Josie's shoulder.

Claire's tears slowly rolled down her cheeks as she watched Josie's do the same. Her child, raw from months of holding her secret inside and now, at the tender age of nineteen, sitting in this room of strangers confessing to them her deepest pain. Her most terrible secret. And these strangers caring so much about her already, enveloping Josie in their arms as if she'd always been part of the group.

The prayers started silently at first with the other folks bowing their heads over folded hands, then the group leader, Marge, started praying out loud, coming over to Josie to place her hand upon her head. A couple other attendees followed suit as they prayed for Josie's physical healing and emotional well-being, concluding with the affirmation that God uses all things for good; that He will give this pain a purpose and the tears will not be shed in vain.

Claire felt a surge of envy; she longed for that same prayer to be prayed over her. For a chance to be accepted because of what she'd done and to be prayed over with such zest that she knew God would certainly hear.

CHAPTER 23

Omaha, NE - Counselor's office – April 1995

After a moment of darkness, Claire found herself in an office with Josie, Nick and another woman sitting before her on overstuffed, eggplant colored armchairs in a room lined with books and what appeared to be a vast collection of angels in every shape, size and medium available, from sun-catchers and sculptures to photos and coasters. Middle-aged with perfectly messy-bun blonde hair, red-rimmed glasses and a light yellow t-shirt that said "coffee and Jesus make life bearable" in bright orange letters, the counselor's personality was pretty much summed up in Claire's ten-second moment of observation. A trait that Claire found herself envying. *Oh to be so open and visible. So peaceful with who you are and what you love.*

"The question isn't necessarily 'why did this happen to me?,'" the counselor was saying. "But rather, 'now that this happened, what am I going to do about it?'" She crossed her legs before continuing. "You can choose how you react and you can choose if you're going to trust God to handle it or if you're going to be resentful and angry, letting the situation ruin your life."

Josie groaned in frustration. "Yea I know. But it's one thing to forgive the guy that raped me cuz I never have to see him again. Hopefully. God willing. But my mom...," Josie explained to the counselor, her voice edged with hostility.

"Oh my goodness. Jacob?" Claire said to the boy, whipping her head around to look at him with surprise. "What is this?"

"It was part of her healing journey. You wondered if she was ever angry." he said, motioning toward the scene before them. "Now you can see for yourself."

"I don't think she even thinks she did anything wrong." Josie continued. She closed her eyes and raised her face to the ceiling, sighing deeply. "I mean, after it was over she just acted like nothing happened.

She was more distant than normal but basically treated me the same as always, like killing a baby wasn't the most terrible thing a person could do." Her voice had raised a notch and her cheeks were beginning to flush.

Claire looked down at her own feet, refusing to look into her daughter's face. *I'm not ready to face this.* She cleared her throat and took a deep breath. *Geez Claire. Twelve years of denial and you're not still ready to face it?*

"She told me to take it easy for a couple weeks to heal up and she worked crazy hours, taking extra shifts and doing more volunteer work for the church and whoever else." She waved her hands in the air indicating she didn't care where her mother had been, it wasn't with her daughter and that's what mattered. "I hardly saw her between then and when I left for college. I think she was avoiding me then, like she blamed *me* for it all, ya know, and now I'm avoiding her because I'm angry." Josie rested her eyes in some distant corner of the room, oblivious to Nick's presence beside her. She seemed to be concentrating on her breathing; probably preventing the anger from consuming her and saying something she truly would regret.

I'm glad she's got more self-restraint than I do. Thought Claire. *I'd have thrown a book across the room by now. Or just walked out and dealt with it by myself.*

"Have you tried to talk to her about this stuff?" the counselor asked, patiently waiting for her response. Josie's breathing was ragged. She took a deep breath then held it for a whole minute, forcing her heartbeat to slow down while she found the courage to continue.

"Oh yea, I've tried, for sure." Her voice was flat and calm. "I called her a couple times when I first got to college, out of obligation, really, to let her know I'd seen my grandparents, my dad's parents, and was settled into the dorms, but those conversations were all surface talk and she seemed to be in a hurry to get off the phone." She sighed heavily. "But at least I tried." She smiled at Nick, indicating her sincerity in attempting to take the high road. "And so I started writing letters to her just as a way to journal what I was thinking, feeling, processing…" She cleared her throat. "And I've written to her just about every month since then, telling her about my life. My journey into adulthood. About us." She squeezed Nick's hand. "About what God is doing in my life and how He's using my past to develop my future and my career. But she's never, not once, replied to any of my letters or even mentioned them the handful of times we actually did speak on the phone."

"Maybe she's ashamed," the counselor offered, "or embarrassed."

"Or simply doesn't care about me anymore." Her face showed the deep pain she felt inside and Claire winced at the accusation.

"That's impossible Josie. You're an amazing woman who would give her left arm if it meant helping someone else out." Nick interjected.

"Is that what they mean when they say "Hey! Give me a hand!"? She managed a giggle at her silliness.

Nick rolled his eyes, "I love your sense of humerus. Haha! Get it? The humerus bone?" he pretended to fall off the chair in fits of fake laughter.

Claire couldn't help but laugh along with the two teens, admiring how much they loved each other and were so comfortable together, joking even in the midst of the serious nature of the conversation. She'd had closeness with her husband Alan but nothing like these two had, and she certainly had not witnessed that between her own parents. But now, watching her daughter glowing with admiration for this young man, she beamed with pride and thankfulness that Josie had such a promising relationship at such a young age.

"She does care," the counselor interjected with seriousness despite her smirk, getting the duo back on course. "From what you've shared with me, yes, she definitely had been tougher on you at times, but that's to be expected based on what you learned about *her* parents. Her father especially. Do you agree with that?"

Josie nodded. "Yea. I get that."

"On that note also, there are patterns of behavior that can be passed down from generation to generation. Abuse, whether it's physical or emotional or whatever, or even continual negativity, yelling instead of talking through things. You get what I'm saying." The counselor spoke with her hands, which Claire respected as a trait she herself possessed. "It sounds like that's what your mother learned in her developmental years at home and then, after your dad died, she resorted back to those learned behaviors as a means to cope with his death and the loss of her own parents and brothers. Does that make sense?"

"Yea, of course."

"It also sounds like she is angry with herself for poor choices she made in high school and she may be denying herself happiness now because of the guilt she still feels. Her insecurities over the past are manifesting as vanity and a hard shell and ill behavior toward you and others."

"I agree. That makes sense. But it still hurts."

"It sure does. And I'm not defending her actions or condoning her attitude toward you at all, but I'm saying that by learning about her and understanding where she's coming from, you can start to view her through eyes of compassion. You can see her not as an adult tyrant, per se, but as a hurting teenager who acted out of confusion, anger and immaturity. You ultimately can see her through the eyes of Jesus, and that makes all the difference."

Josie exhaled deeply as though she'd been holding her breath. "Wow! That breaks my heart." Tears welled up in the young woman's eyes and she squeezed Nick's hand tightly. "She must have been so sad to leave her family. And by force too. Even though my dad loved her… but to not have a mother to lean on, or her younger brothers… I mean, she missed out on their entire lives." Sobs racked her body as waves of remorseful compassion overwhelmed her.

Nick held her tight until she caught her breath again. "Yea, at seventeen that's a lot to deal with. Then to have you at such a young age too," he said.

He shook his head and clasped his heart with his hand. "I can't imagine being disowned by her family, moving across the country, not knowing anyone but her husband, having a baby, then having her husband die, then moving, again, halfway across the country to a place where she had to start over from scratch. Wow! That's a lot to handle.

And I'm a guy! You ladies are more sensitive and vulnerable and feel things more deeply."

"I know. Right?" Josie said, wiping her tears with a tissue. "It's heartbreaking to think of my mom like that. I'm sad that I didn't sympathize with her more when I was growing up."

"But you didn't know." the counselor stated. "And even if you had known, nothing could have helped her deal with the disownment or your dad's death. Those are things she would have had to process in her own way, with the help of friends and counselors or pastoral leadership. But I tell ya, having her family around sure would have helped a great deal after your dad died. Just to have an extra set of hands to help with you, as a toddler. To give her advice or a mommy break."

"No wonder she stayed so busy. I think if she had slowed down for any length of time she probably would have fallen into depression and given up completely." Josie said.

"It's entirely possible." The counselor agreed, sitting back in her chair and crossing her legs. "Sometimes the survival instinct works like that. But it's only when we face our problems, face the pain, and give our minds and bodies the time and resources they need to sort it out, can we heal and forgive others, or ourselves, and really, truly be at peace." She closed her notebook and put the lid on her pen, setting the items on the table beside her.

"We can't run from our problems, otherwise we'll never stop. We'll always relocate where we live, change schools or jobs, get divorced, stay in the same patterns, over and over again. But if we stop when a problem arises, turn and face it. Examine it, be honest with ourselves and God, repent, if needed, seek counseling, pray, change some of our habits or behaviors or attitudes... well, that's when the real living starts. That's when we can live in freedom from the fear of failure, because we know that every situation presents us with an opportunity to learn and grow and draw closer to God."

She paused to sip her coffee before continuing. "We are adaptable people, but we also need to be responsible enough to humble ourselves and face making some changes within ourselves at times. Some people avoid that like the plague and others, like yourself, have a support system, even if it's just Nick." She winked at the young man. "Someone that encourages us to keep going and seek help, cuz, let's be honest, we can't always do things on our own."

"I should forgive her but sometimes I'm so angry I just wanna go to her house and start yelling at her. I mean, I understand that she was mad that I got pregnant but she acted so rashly and didn't even seem to stop and think about what she was doing to me." Josie said.

"Yea. I hear that." the counselor said. "Sometimes the anger of a moment takes control and blocks out common sense and kindness. Even though we may know what is right and wrong, we still only see the situation we're in and oftentimes act out in aggression or anger. It all just leads us down a dark road of sin and regret. But as Christians, we gotta remember that forgiveness isn't for us to think about, Josie, it's commanded of us in the Bible." [1]

Claire stood silent, saying and thinking nothing, just absorbing the counselor's words and letting them sink deeply into her heart. She felt her shoulders relax as another layer of hardness was lifted.

Nick tenderly stroked the back of her hand with his thumb, encouraging her silently. "Forgiveness doesn't make the pain go away or make us forget what happened. It makes it possible for us to let the bitterness go from inside us and start to heal," he said. "It's a promise we make to ourselves and God to not hold onto the anger, but instead lay it at the foot of the cross."

She nodded her head in agreement.

"You don't have to see your mom right now or talk to her necessarily, that relationship will take time to heal, but you can pray about it and tell God that you forgive her and ask Him to help you release the resentment every time it pops up." He said, nudging her shoulder. "Every day a little step forward, okay?"

"Okay."

CHAPTER 24

The In-between Place

Jacob looked at Claire's face; moist tracks showing on her cheeks. "Tell me about the letters that she wrote to you."

A small frown flickered across her brow as she looked at him. *He really was going to dig all the dirt out of her life wasn't he?* She shrugged her shoulders and tried to distract him by asking questions about the fish he never seemed to catch despite his constant attempts, but he would not be deterred.

Claire sat on the cool, long grass, crossing her legs in front of her. "Josie is right. She writes to me all the time." She touched a velvety stem of grass and began caressing it between her fingertips. "About once every six or eight weeks I get something from her. A card or a letter. But after the first few arrived I never read them."

"Why not?" Jacob said.

Claire shrugged nonchalantly. "Pride, I guess." She tossed a shade-cooled rock into the water and plucked another from the river bank. "Or jealousy maybe. Embarrassment. My selfishness." The list of excuses could have continued but she paused, hoping Jacob would accept her story thus far and give her permission to stop.

He only nodded and raised his eyebrows, silently encouraging her to keep talking.

"So her first couple letters arrived not long after she went to college and they explained to me that she was deeply hurt and very angry about the abortion. She told me that she didn't know if she could ever forgive me and said she was glad to be out of the house and two hundred miles away from me so that she didn't have to deal with my "pessimistic and overbearing presence" anymore." She air-quoted the phrase as her shoulders slumped forward in defeat at the remembrance of the pain those words had caused her all those years ago. Pain she deserved, by all means, but terrible to own up to nonetheless. "The second letter was pretty much the same. I think it mentioned her and Nick and maybe some new church they were going to. I don't remember exactly."

That's a lie. I remember it all.

"But this I do know." She paused. "That her words were painfully true and I didn't want to listen to her preaching to me. So I stopped reading the letters." Her voice was soft and heavy with regret now that she knew that Josie had been keeping her informed of her college experiences, including her evolving relationship with Nick, and her healing process. How wonderful it would have been to know her daughter was doing well and was actually happy all these years.

"I wish I'd had Alan longer; to help me heal like Nick did for Josie," she whispered. "He was so good for me. Strong and patient. I think we could have had a really great life together."

Jacob stayed in silence as her pain spoke.

"I suppose maybe, if I'd not been so stubborn, I could have found some good friends to lean on. Maybe someone from church. Or a neighbor lady or something. Someone who could have been a sounding board for me. But I was so bitter that God took away my family and Alan, that I kind of did the whole *"screw you God, I'll do this myself"* approach to life."

She shuffled her feet and took a ragged breath. "Now it's pretty obvious I messed that up, huh?" she said thickly.

"God knows your heart.[1] He knows your pain and He saw you trying. He saw your struggles and yes, He could have blessed you a great deal through friendships with neighbors and at church, and Josie for that matter, if you'd made different choices. But here's the best news!" he exclaimed. "It's not too late. He can, and will, use all those choices and situations for good even if it takes longer than other people."

"I'm a slow learner." she said, tucking her long hair behind her ear.

"It's okay. Life is full of lessons. Sometimes we learn them fast and sometimes it takes a long time. And sometimes God does that for a reason, you know, to make us into the person He wants us to be. The character of Christ that He wants us to have doesn't just show up overnight, it might take many years."

Claire nodded. Understanding the boy's implications.

"Did you know that God created the garden of Eden *and* the wilderness that the Israelites wandered in for forty years?"

His obvious question took her by surprise. "Well, yeah. Of course He did. That's a silly question."

"So the garden was kind of like being on a really great vacation. Life was good there. All the needs of Adam and Eve were met. God was with them. It was paradise." 2

"And your point is?"

"But then you have the Israelites who were rescued from Egypt by Moses and promised, by God, some land to live in. The Promised Land. You know the story, right?" He looked at her with inquisitive eyes.

Claire couldn't help but smile at Jacob's innocent remarks and admire how familiar his features looked. Inherited features. She nodded.

"The Israelites had seen God perform lots of miracles, like the plagues that led to their deliverance from Egypt and the pillar of clouds and fire that led them through the desert. He also gave them manna that fell out of the sky and quails each day to eat, but they still complained. Then when the spies told what the Promised Land looked like and how big the people were that lived there, they got scared. They didn't think God could help them defeat those people and take the land that God said was already theirs so He made them stay in the wilderness for forty years." 3

She narrowed her eyes at him, wondering where he was going with this story.

"So that's all just proof that God gives paradise *and* He gives wilderness experiences. He created the Garden *and* He created the desert. Life can't all be fun and vacations, sometimes there are trials and loneliness."

"I definitely know about all that."

"But sometimes it's God's will that we go through times of trials. It tests our faith and strengthens our relationship with God. It makes us more patient, or loving, or compassionate, or all sorts of other things that are good. Things that make us more like Christ."

"It's difficult." She choked on her words. "I mean, to be alone during those times."

Jacob held her hand. "Even Jesus went through forty days of temptations in the wilderness.[4] But God was with him. Just like He was with you all these years. He's been trying to get your attention, just like the Israelites, He's been giving you chances to reunite with Him but other stuff distracts you and causes you to doubt His goodness."

The truth of his words was undeniable. She was incredibly guilty of pushing God aside and acting on her own accord. Behaving vainly, speaking harshly, seeking external validation instead of focusing on developing a character that resembles Christ. *No wonder I've been left alone to figure it out, who else would want to be around me?*

"So the Israelites ultimately reached the Promised Land. Right?" she inquired, already knowing the answer.

He nodded. "Yep. But only after the generation of people who doubted God's promises died."

"Oh geez."

"I know. That's pretty harsh. But they were walking by sight, not faith.[5] They let satan fill their minds with questions, thinking that all hope was lost, that *they* were lost and God had forgotten about them. They let themselves be overcome with complaining and doubts instead of staying strong in their faith that God would keep His promises. You see, He offered them a chance, many chances actually, and lots of years to stop complaining and turn back to Him, but they didn't. They continued to live in defeat and complained amongst themselves and God grew frustrated with them so much that He didn't let them go into the Promised Land for forty more years."

"Seems they were just like most people are these days." *Like me.*

"You see, Claire, God has no problem leading us into a wilderness time in our lives or allowing us to wander in there by our own actions and free will. The wilderness can be a place where we may feel hopeless or lonely or desperate but He's always there with us. He doesn't force His presence on us but rather longs for us to choose to have a relationship with Him. At the same time, He's got no problem leaving us in the wilderness for as long as it takes us to realize we need *Him*. We need Christ and His grace."

She exhaled, long and slow, contemplating his words. "Yea, I admit I'm there. That wilderness has been my home for quite some time now."

"But you're not meant to live there Claire. It's supposed to be, and hopefully is, temporary. There's a way out. There's a Promised Land He's got prepared for you but He's gonna let you discover that any place in your life that isn't focused on God, doesn't last."

Guilty as she was for living in doubt and rebellion most of her life, letting herself be overcome with doubt and negativity, she knew millions of other people in the world were in the same boat. Seeking external validation for their looks or deeds. Searching for love in meaningless, shallow relationships that led to even more rejection and loneliness. Shaping their worlds around what was expected of them: high school, college, marriage, kids, work your butt off, retire and hope to have a little energy and health left to enjoy your last 2 decades of life, instead of around God's will for their lives.

"If we all would put God first, we could all avoid a heck of a lot of heartbreak, huh? I know I could have." She rubbed her temples, fending off some building tension. "I was even raised in the church and taught what was right and I still messed it all up. Imagine what those people who don't have a loving family or church to attend go through."

Her heart ached knowing how much her life would have been different, better, had she made better choices as a teenager. If she had truly listened to the sermons preached on Sundays and applied their lessons to her everyday life, instead of running around behind her folks' backs, partying and making out with guys. Seeking external validation to disguise the emptiness she felt inside. An emptiness that only her Creator could fill, as she was discovering now. Her unrepentant attitude was taking its toll on her mind and body, hardening her heart against God. Pushing her further and further out. After so many years in the wilderness, she was willing to end her own life to prevent the mound of pain and remorse from collapsing and burying her completely.

"I hope my Promised Land is still available." she whispered.

CHAPTER 25

A slight swishing sound filled the air as the cattails brushed against one another like two lovers in a tango dance. From her vantage point on the hillside, Claire watched their brown heads bob and weave around each other as if flirting was their only means by which to communicate. The sun was never seen, but its light shone abundantly, constantly, in all directions. The sun never set here, not in this In-between place, as she was referring to it in her mind. So it radiated above her now and beckoned her to use its illumination to shed light on her shadows.

She could feel the tug of the Holy Spirit, stronger than it had been these past several years. Ignorance is bliss until ignorance no longer holds up its end of the bargain and bliss evaporates; what remains behind is truth. And truth, she knew, was hard to hide from. It always emerges. It always shows its face eventually. It always forces us to either face it back or lose part of ourselves to its power. If we choose the latter, then truth exits but leaves denial in its place; internally destroying us little by little in a way that no healthy eating or daily exercise can heal.

And so Claire found herself face to face with the truth once more. *Tell me,* the inner voice beckoned. Her chest was locked up, feeling hard as stone as she fought the calling. She'd been in this place before, several times, but always managed to push the voice away and leave its insistence a memory for a short time before it returned, requesting that she listen, hopeful that she would.

The battle between free will and submission is strong and profoundly difficult. Easier to submit to free will than to submit to the Creator's call to repentance and a changed heart, mind and lifestyle. But easier doesn't mean pain free. The only way to true peace is to come clean, face the truth and be honest before the Creator.

Oh God, her mind started to reel, *I don't even know where to start. I can't even remember the last time I really, openly talked to you in silent prayer, let alone out-loud.* Her Catholic upbringing was full of routine; pomp and circumstance; obligations and formal procedures.

Personalization was optional, like many religions are, and hers was missing. Once upon a time perhaps it existed, when Alan was alive, but since that hot summer twelve years ago it'd grown cold and hard. Giving up on God because you don't feel He's listening, or hearing, or answering prayers, or even cares is one thing, but feeling as though God has given up on you is entirely different.

CHAPTER 26

"You know, Josie prays a lot." Jacob told her a few hours later as they walked through the trees lining the south river bank. The birds were chirping like a Sunday morning choir and Claire knew she'd never heard anything more beautiful in her life. "She thanks God for her healing and she prays for your heart and mind to be healed too."

Claire was deep in thought, mindlessly twirling a piece of brome grass between her fingers while its counterparts brushed against her legs. "That's why she leads those support groups, right?" She looked over at him. "It's therapy for her too, to help others find peace and forgiveness."

He nodded and smiled. "She's seeing that silver lining; that thing God does with bad situations. She's pursuing the good that He's brought out of her pain and she's allowing herself to be used by Him to help others. She understands that He never lets anything bad happen to His followers without turning it into something good later on."

"What good has come out of it for me though? I've been overly miserable for the past twelve years and have a dysfunctional, ruined relationship with my daughter."

"Have you been miserable because of God being God, or because of your own choices?" he countered, stopping in his tracks as he waited for a response.

With a faint sense of irritation Claire realized this young boy was reprimanding her. And although it was in the most tactful, innocent way, it still stung. For the past twelve years she'd been attending church weekly, sometimes twice a week, taking holy communion once a month and giving of her time and money to the Church. But she was no closer to God than the day she chose to push Him aside for personal pleasure at the age of fifteen.

She turned to face him. "I regret a lot of things I've done. Choices I've made. Attitudes and what not. I guess I don't understand why I can't find peace or even be happy anymore."

"Regret is not the same as repentance."[1]

She scowled openly at him.

"The pain of past regrets can cause us to continue to make poor decisions. It's basically self-destruction because we're unhealed and damaged and trying to push through life with a broken leg, which is what it seems like you've been experiencing. But the good news is that regret can also be used to draw us closer to God, through true repentance. That's like finally going to the doctor to get a cast on your broken leg so it can heal properly."

"I like that analogy Jacob. Thank you." She smiled at the boy, grateful for his insight and amazed by his wisdom. *He truly has a connection to God in a way I can't explain.*

"You see, we can regret a lot of things we do or say, thinking that by feeling bad about it we'll be forgiven, but if we don't confess those things to the one we offended, and seek forgiveness and learn from it, then it's kinda pointless."

"But the Lord has heard it all from me. I tell Him my struggles and needs and constantly pray for help."

Jacob interrupted, "Have you told him about the abortion?"

CHAPTER 27

July 1993

"What? NO!" Josie defended herself. "You can't do this?" Claire's mind traveled back to the day she and Josie drove across the state line. The memory was so engraved in her mind, even despite her attempts to dislodge it still played out before her like it happened yesterday.

"I can and I will. The choice is not yours Josie." Claire said sternly, eyes never leaving the windshield with its black wipers swishing the moisture away from her line of sight. A fine mist coated their small two-door Chevy Beretta as it sped down the interstate. The fog hung low, making visibility limited.

Josie had been oblivious to the schemes her mother was plotting until this morning, before the sun rose, Claire jolted Josie from sleep, instructing her to dress in sweatpants and get in the car in ten minutes, not revealing their destination or purpose for nearly a half an hour.

"It's murder, Mom." Her shrill voice was frantic with fear when she was informed they were going to a discrete clinic to terminate the pregnancy.

Claire's expression was stone cold, completely indifferent to her daughter's pleas. "If you have this baby it'll ruin your life. I guarantee it. And besides that, do you know what this'll do to us in this town? Do you have any idea what the church will say about this crap?!" Her question was rhetorical, not that Josie had an answer for her anyhow. "We'll be shunned and looked down on for the rest of our lives."

"It won't ruin my life," she pleaded.

"Oh really? So you can just forget about college and... and you can tell your friends that you've decided to be like your mother, a night shift worker that has no social life or hobbies because of her kid." Claire's animosity did not slip by Josie, whose heart could nearly be heard breaking at the bitter confession. The judgment was thick and pungent in the small car.

Josie shook her head, not sure what to make of her mother's comments. "No. I can give it up for adoption and then start college. It'll only delay me by one semester, Mom." Her voice flat, the energy quickly leaving her as her mind struggled to understand how callused her mother was being.

Her mother glared at her. "Oh really? So that'll work just fine, huh Josie? You can just hang out in the house for the next eight months so no one finds out about this? No church, no grocery store, no mowing the lawn or even checking the mail cuz god forbid someone might drive by and see you?" Her sarcasm was so vehement it echoed through the car. "You're getting an abortion!"

Josie didn't move. Didn't breathe. That word echoed through the car like it was the Grand Canyon bouncing off the roof, the floorboards and windows then back to her broken heart.

"It's murder Mom. You know that it's murder." Her voice was stern. "A baby's heart starts beating before a woman misses her period; before she even knows she's pregnant. This is a human being!"

"This is not your choice, Josephine!"

"It's my body and it's my baby! It doesn't matter how it was conceived, it's still *my* baby. I can give it up for adoption." Her mother tried to silence her with a stern look. "Come'on Mom, I'll go away somewhere until it's born. I'll stay with friends or relatives somewhere far away from here so no one will know about it. Please mom! We can't do this!" She put her hand on her mother's arm, pleading with her tears and soul.

Claire rolled her eyes, fed up with her daughter's pleas and nagging. *Can't keep a child that was conceived out of wedlock. Rape or no rape.* She still wasn't convinced she believed Josie on that point. *The girl is probably slutting around behind my back.* They were not going through with this pregnancy.

Claire pulled her arm from Josie's grasp, "We are doing this. In a few hours it's all gonna be over and then we can get our lives back." They drove in silence for several miles, the swishing of the wipers the only sound between them.

"You can recover at home, then pack your stuff up and leave for college. Until then we just keep our mouths shut about this whole deal and then we can keep the embarrassment to a minimum. News of this gets out and we'll have to change churches and social circles… probably just move out of state is what I'd do." she said, thinking out loud more than she should have.

Going against everything she knew to be right, Josie dared challenge her mother, "Are you serious? You're more concerned about being embarrassed than you are about committing murder?! This is a child! Your grandchild…"

"It is not a child that can be brought into this world. God won't allow that sort of creation conceived by lust and sin to live. He'll probably make you miscarry it anyway as punishment for your actions." Claire said.

"I was not sinning or lusting, I was raped! Why can't you believe me?" Josie was beside herself with confusion at her mother's lack of trust in her. Their relationship hadn't been super close because her mother worked a lot, but they talked easily when they were together, worked side-by-side keeping their home and little acreage in shape, and didn't argue. Ever. Until now.

"Your sin has led you into this pit and I'm going to get you out. Someday you can thank me for allowing you to still have a life and go to college and not be tied down with a kid." Claire motioned with her hands for Josie to open the glove box. Josie complied. "Give me those." Indicating the pack of menthol cigarettes and lighter. Josie's jaw dropped as she slowly reached in for the items, putting them to her mother's trembling hands. She'd never known her mother to smoke; had no idea that was even an option.

"This topic is no longer open for discussion." Claire pulled a menthol from the package and lit it up, cracking the window slightly to allow the smoke to escape. Claire found herself wishing she were smoke and could so easily be removed from this situation, from this car and task ahead of her. She let the effects of the cigarette wash over her, enjoying the slight buzz that rushed through her body, intensified by the infrequency of the ritual. This was a habit she didn't entertain that often, just after an abnormally stressful work day or when her daughter showed up pregnant. She turned the music up louder to drown out the voice in her head that told her *this isn't right. You know this isn't right.*

Pushing the accelerator further down, she inched the odometer higher to expedite the day, anxious to get home and back to normal.

Josie sat in stoney silence, forehead against the pane, her eyes fixated on the high-line wires and fence poles zipping past her window. The dark earthen fields displayed their canvases of green in tidy rows that stretched out from her gaze. To Claire she looked like she wanted to die right where she sat. Shallow breaths labored in her chest and tears rolled down her red, swollen cheeks, evidence of multiple nights spent in restless agony.

Claire's demeanor was stoney as well, not from emotion or turmoil but from anger at her daughter having put her in the situation in the first place. The redness of her own eyes was covered by perfectly applied makeup; her hair neatly french braided with any loose strands tucked behind her ears or held in place by bobby pins. Lip gloss shining, she stared ahead, faking ignorance of Josie's turmoil.

Claire was allowed to be in the procedural room with Josie but chose not to partake. Waiting in the lobby instead, looking at old copies of *Time* and *Good Housekeeping* and trying to memorize the 'tips and tricks to looking more youthful' until the nurse called for her to come and get their patient. Josie had laid on the back seat of the car and sobbed all the way home.

"You can kill a child but you can't let me ride in a car without a seatbelt on?!" she yelled at her mother when told to buckle up. Claire realized her once gentle and respectful daughter was now gone.

The wind knew that day, and the sky also. It was late June but cold gusts of wind bit at the brome grass atop the river bottom hills and blew down through the ravines as fierce as a winter squall. It shook the front window pane of their house, the loose one Claire had intended to fix for the past year but never seemed to get around to, and seeped under the door. Later that evening rain drops, hard as tacks, hit the roof in constant reprimand as though punishing Claire's actions.

Claire stood in the kitchen for hours, her breath fogging the front window, trying not to think about what just transpired that morning, but finding that with every breath her heart was cracking open a bit more, revealing unpleasantries that were best left in the dark. She tried holding her breath; that didn't work. She could lose herself in a bottle of wine but knew it would only give her a massive headache and thus another problem.

It was as though a giant hand were clamping her heart and squeezing. Squeezing out all the shock, the anger, the logic so that it oozed outside and ran down the front steps like worms after a spring rain. She vowed to herself that dreary afternoon to never speak of that day's events ever again; she would instead forget them. Repression could be successful if repeated often enough.

CHAPTER 28

The In-between Place

Claire had ignored that still inner voice on that first day and had been fairly successful ever since, although it never fully went away, lodging instead deep in her heart, repressed and simmering. It was out of her mind at least and that's all she cared about, for the first several years. During that time Claire thought she was being tested in patience and tolerance. After seventeen years of being the mother to an obedient and respectful child, this was her big parental test. Most parents were tested by their kids on a weekly, or daily, basis so Claire knew she'd gotten off pretty lucky with such a great kid.

But the voice came more and more frequently now, disrupting her dreams, her working hours, her general peace and quiet. There was no escape from the heaviness laid upon her heart that was wreaking havoc on her body and life. It started with headaches and shoulder tensions, which she pawned off as stress from work and took muscle relaxants for when it got too painful to sleep. Then it was high blood pressure, easily fixable with pills from her family practitioner, then knee pain that was so intense it made her give up her lovely garden and brooder house full of chickens a few years back.

Concerned about walking in public, especially at church, without limping from pain, Claire took pain meds well in advance of putting on her heels and dress so by all outward appearances she was perfectly healthy. There were times while using the stairs at church when her knee locked up, shooting pain through her hip and into her lower back with such intensity she nearly toppled over. She covered those moments quickly by pretending she had an itch on her calf or shoulder, anything to get her mind off her agony and distract whomever might be watching her, observing for flaws.

The restless nights and dreams of babies crying in dark hallways haunted her for multiple months after the incident until she discovered if she left the radio on in her bedroom and took a sleeping pill before bedtime she could avoid most of those unpleasantries.

But God was calling to her, convicting her, despite all of her distractions and attempts to cover the pain, and He wouldn't let her rest until the issue was dealt with. It made her laugh some days and cry others, depending on how much spare time she had.

"I know I've been pushing Him away." Claire brushed her thumb over a smooth rock as they sat near the tree stump. "I keep thinking that if enough time passes He'll just forget about it." She glanced at Jacob, loving how the breeze picked at his dark hair. "But if I can't forget, how can He?"

"The Bible says that the wages of sin is death.[1] Guess it'd be easier to be good people if the consequences of our sins happened immediately." Jacob waded into the clear water, giggling at the way the water tickled his feet.

Claire's eyes widened at the concept of dying instantly as soon as a singular sin was committed.

"But He doesn't just mean death, like real death," he said, looking back at her, "which *could* happen, but it could be the death of a dream we had, or loss of our money, or death of will power or joy, or loss of a relationship. Instead God lets us use our free will and make our own choices, even if they are unhealthy for us or the people around us. The consequences are there regardless, sometimes stretched out for months or years or a whole lifetime."

A lifetime of consequences. Claire took that personally. She felt she did what she had to do at the time. Circumstances beyond their control were making the rules and she merely played the game, making her moves as she saw fit. *Oh what beautiful lies we tell ourselves when the truth is too ugly to bear.*

With her head down in her hands, Claire felt hot tears seep between her fingers and onto her dress.

"I feel so lost, Jacob. Like my whole life is a mistake and everything I do is wrong."

Jacob kicked water at a nearby fish and laughed as it darted away.

"God knows that. He knows what you need way more than you do. And He doesn't make mistakes. Josie was not a mistake and you were not a mistake and your life isn't a mistake. The Bible says *I knew you before I formed you in your mother's womb."* [2]

"He doesn't make mistakes, huh?" her doubt was evident in her tone. "Okay, but if I hadn't gotten pregnant then my family wouldn't have disowned me and Josie wouldn't have been around to be raped and there would have been no abortion or destruction of our lives. This whole situation never would have happened."

"God didn't make you get pregnant with Josie. You had free will to do whatever you wanted and you chose to be with Alan. That's how you got pregnant."

Claire was offended at the boy's truthful words and opened her mouth to protest, but the conviction in her heart knowing that he was right stopped her. She had made the choice to have sex with Alan before they were married; when she was too young and irresponsible.

"You also made the choice to keep Josie, when adoption was an available option."

"Yea." Was all Claire said, nodding her head. "But Alan wanted her so badly I didn't feel like I could let him down."

"You also chose to make Josie have the abortion even though adoption was an option with her as well."

Claire's head was bowed in embarrassment and shame.

"Okay, so why was I punished for doing what was right?" Wrinkles crossed her forehead as she held back her tears. *I'm so tired of fighting this.* "I mean, I kept my baby and married Alan and I was punished for it. I'm still being punished for it, and dragging Josie down too in the process."

"You weren't punished. There are consequences to sinning and disobeying God." [3]

Her brows furrowed, a silent urge for him to continue before her mouth started speaking out of turn.

"Sin has consequences, even if we are believers. When we are unkind and break someone's trust we can expect that relationship to suffer.

That's a natural consequence of our actions. If we put our trust in people or things other than God, we can expect to be disappointed and frustrated, and sometimes that disappointment and frustration can cause us to sin even further."

"Yea, I understand that."

"We also have to deal with the consequences of the sins of other people."

"People who intentionally hurt others?"

Jacob nodded. "Yep, with their words, or weapons, or neglect. All kinds of stuff."

"Let's not forget what a cruddy world this can be sometimes." Claire said snidely.

"Yea, we live in a fallen world where lots of people give in to evil things and sin rather than do what is loving and right.[4] Problems don't mean God is mad at us or is punishing us, Claire. Sometimes He is angry at us for sinning over and over again and not listening to Him by turning away from wickedness, and other times He's using difficult situations to discipline us. To build perseverance and patience in us."[5]

He sat down beside her, holding her hand tenderly and looking into her eyes.

"Our God is a God of love. He IS love. He's slow to get angry and always ready to forgive us if we cry out to Him and repent."[6,7] He's been patient with you. He doesn't want you to struggle with this anymore and you don't need to fear His anger either cuz He's been knocking on the door, waiting for you to hear Him and respond to His voice. He wants you to choose Him; to be close to Him. He made a way through Jesus and nothing and no one can separate you from His love."[8]

"God's got it all worked out Claire. No matter what." he said.

Her wide green eyes met his. Her surprise was obvious as she caught her breath.

"Those were the last words I heard my husband say to me." Less than two weeks later, she received a knock at the door of their modest two bedroom base house from a man in a sharp khaki colored uniform who, with as much sympathy as he could muster, informed her that her husband had been killed in a military vehicle rollover accident and would not be coming home.

"But you already knew that, didn't you?" she said.

He nodded.

Tears spilled over her cheeks. "I'm so angry, Jacob." Claire whispered, her strength spent. "So mad at myself for being stupid and getting pregnant so young. I'm mad at my family for turning their backs on me, for losing my chance at college and my dreams of a life outside of the Midwest. I'm mad that I had to move to Arizona where it was so damned hot. And then, of all things, Alan had to go and die and leave me even more alone."

Jacob rubbed her shoulder, comforting her with his touch. "In order to get past your anger and grief over what you've lost, you have to understand that you can't undo what was done, neither can you go back and do what was left undone. Unforgiveness keeps us tied to the things that happened in the past and satan can use that to torment your mind and heart, so it's really important that you forgive your parents, and Alan too, even though he's not alive anymore."

He touched her arm. "And you have to forgive yourself Claire, for making choices based on feelings and worldly deceptions instead of God's truth."

"How? It seems impossible," she said.

The boy grinned. "Well, I happen to know that God specializes in impossible things."

She contemplated his words as she kicked off her shoes and stepped into the cool water. *It does tickle!* And she giggled alongside Jacob while silvery fish swam close to their toes as if daring each other to take the first nibble. The experience took her back to the late 1970's when Josie was first taking swimming lessons and Claire would wade in the kiddie pool while the instructor worked with the young girl on holding her breath and exhaling through her nose. On hot summer days the cool water from the pool was a welcomed relief and she relished the time to relax while daydreaming she was on a tropical island wading in the ocean.

Bringing her thoughts back to reality she asked a question she had been pondering for hours. "Do you think Josie ever wished that guy dead?" she said, her chest tightening at the thought.

Jacob gave her a questioning look. "*That* guy?" he asked.

She nodded, not wanting to give him any credit by saying his name out loud.

"I'll show you."

CHAPTER 29

Omaha, NE - Summer 2001

The uneven terrain of the cobblestone streets in Omaha's Old Market district were beneath their feet, the multi-story buildings rising up around them with quaint coffee shops and boutiques tucked between their sturdy walls. Claire admired a guitar player's music as he entertained passersby just ten feet from them. Josie caught her eye, walking down the sidewalk toward them, a book in one hand and her purse in the other with a look of serene calm on her face, upturned now toward the warm sun.

Getting her bearings in the area, Claire turned and noted the blue door of the support group's location across the intersection from where they stood, its color hard to forget from her and Jacob's previous trip here.

"She's probably going to work, huh?" Claire said.

"BOOMER!" a man's voice yelled from somewhere unseen, causing Claire to jump in surprise.

Claire witnessed her daughter instantly tense up at the sound of the name. She dropped the book and stopped dead in her tracks; a look of panic upon her face.

"Oh no," said Claire, assuming the worst situation possible was going to play out before them. "He's not here, is he?" Looking around she didn't see anything but the normal locals and tourists milling about, minding their own business.

"Boomer!" came the voice again.

Josie backed up into the shadow of an awning, pressing her back against the brick building, clutching her purse to her chest. She was visibly shaking.

Just then a large dog, black with white splotches across its back, bolted across the intersection, its blue leash trailing behind it. A car honked, then another, as the animal narrowly avoided being hit by a delivery truck.

"You dumb dog!" a man said loudly, rushing past Jacob and Claire. "I'm gonna kill ya when I catch ya!" He put his hand up in a 'stop' motion, causing an oncoming car to squeal its tires, as he ran as hard as he could down the cobblestone street anxiously pursuing the disobedient dog.

With the commotion past them, Claire turned toward Josie again. The young woman, once realizing that Boomer was a dog and not the man of whom she cowered from, breathed a huge sigh of relief and walked, on trembling legs, to pick up her book.

Josie clutched it to her chest and closed her eyes, not caring who heard her pray aloud. "Lord, that was a close call." She took a deep breath before continuing. "Thank you for protecting me from an encounter with that man. I put my trust in You and thank you for reminding me that I am loved and safe. I have chosen to forgive him and don't want to lose my inner peace and joy by holding onto the past. By your grace, I don't feel the need to hold a grudge against him or hold any hate in my heart. Keep me from the temptation to give in to vengeful thoughts and anger. I release it all to you in Jesus' name."

Jacob turned to Claire as they watched Josie walk away. "She still has struggles. Everyone does. But she knows the One who heals and helps her is always by her side, ready to give strength when she is weak or scared."

"She's so brave," said Claire.

"She is, but she's also dependent upon the Lord more than she is upon anything or anyone else. Forgiving that man doesn't mean she won't get caught up in the angry thoughts or memories of what happened. Forgiving him means she's promised herself not to let the hate or pain rule her mind or heart. In the same way, God forgives us. He promised, through Jesus' sacrifice, to not hold our sins against us."

CHAPTER 30

The In-Between Place

Jacob held Claire's hand and led her along the riverside path, to a meadow filled with the most gorgeous wildflowers she'd ever seen. Bright yellows, vibrant pinks and blooms of lavender Pasque, the State flower, covered the ground and seemed to worship the warm sunlight above. Waving to and fro in a dance of adoration. Their displays of radiance were almost too much to look at directly; so majestic were their colors.

She was deep in thought, paying no attention to the rabbits and skunks scooting through the meadow or the deer drinking from the cool river.

"I know you feel that life hasn't been fair. That you didn't get dealt a fair hand with your dad, or Alan's death. But God never said life would be fair. He sometimes allows bad things to happen to good people to strengthen their faith, and to prove His faithfulness and love toward them." [1]

Claire's thoughtful look of consideration encouraged him to continue. "Do you remember Job?"

She nodded. "God allowed Satan to take everything away from Job, including his ten kids, his land, home, and health, thinking that Job would hate God for the tragedies and turn away from his faith. But Job remained faithful, knowing that God would restore all that was lost or taken from him." [2]

"Most people *would* give up and curse God and get angry and resentful. Just like I did." Her voice faltered as she thought of what her own response had been toward her Creator at the loss of her family and loved ones. Many years of resentment had built up, layer upon layer, in her heart and mind to the point that God was a distant helper that didn't really want to help her after all.

"Just like Job, Josie trusted God's plan for her life even though she didn't understand it at first. It took her many long months of intense counseling and seeking after God's heart for her to realize that His plan was playing out before her eyes."

"You know," Claire said, "I'm really envious. I wish I'd figured that out sooner."

"That's one of the great things about God. He's full of wonderful surprises and has done great works in Josie's life. I hate to say it again, but you'd know about them already if you had read Josie's letters."

Claire shook her head in disappointment. "I know, I failed on that one."

"True, you didn't read the letters cuz of some personal and painful reasons, but did you ever think that maybe God was in that situation too?"

"Huh?" She looked confused.

"That maybe He was waiting for you to hear His voice and draw close to Him *first*, before He let you in on the life that Josie found?"

CHAPTER 31

Omaha, NE – Summer 1995

Josie sat alone, her nervous fingers tracing the lip of a coffee cup as she glanced out the rain-streaked window.

Claire looked around inside the cafe and recognized it as being "Dollie's Diner", the oldest diner in the Old Market district of Omaha and a place she and her family frequented when Claire was a young teenager. It still looked exactly the same. Short, red vinyl topped stools were lined up in front of the countertop while booths lined the outer walls. Waitresses in short sleeved, red and white gingham dresses skirted around pouring bottomless cups of coffee and delivering plates heaped with hot food to regulars and newbies alike. *Just like I remember.*

Caught off guard by a rumble of thunder, Claire turned toward the window and caught a glimpse of the woman at the same time Josie did. She was wearing a hooded red jacket that fell nearly to her knees and she walked as quickly as a lady could in high heels; her black nylons a striking contrast to the red shoes. A bell dinged as she entered the diner, a trigger for the waitresses to simultaneously speak their *"Welcome to Dollie's"* greeting.

The woman shrugged out of her jacket and shook it slightly, dislodging any remaining droplets to the carpet below, before looking at her surroundings.

"Oh my goodness." Claire gasped, nearly falling over. Jacob squeezed her hand. "Mother?" Tears welled up as Claire watched her mother, still so slim and beautiful with her neatly curled hair, partially gray now after all the years, walk toward Josie, her handbag clutched in front of her.

"Hello dear. You must be Josie." The woman said, reaching out her slender hand to the girl. "You look just like Claire..." Her voice faltered.

"Hi." said Josie, clearing her throat. "Yes I've heard that before."

The two stared at each other, hands clasped, as if in a time warp.

Neither seemed to want to stop the moment of bonding that was clearly occurring.

"Can I get you some coffee, Ma'am?" the waitress said, her southern accent revealing that the gal certainly wasn't from Nebraska.

Remembering her manners, the elder woman spoke first. "Yes please. That would be delightful."

She gingerly sat in the booth opposite Josie, placing her handbag beside her and clasping her hands in her lap.

"What am I supposed to call you?" Josie blurted out, blushing in the process.

"She's so nervous." said Claire, unable to fully grasp what she was witnessing.

"Well, let's see. You can call me Miss Eleanor, as the ladies at church call me, or Ellie, or grandma." She paused, a look of anxious anticipation on her face. "I suppose that would also be appropriate."

"It's just so weird meeting you." said Josie. "I mean, I didn't even know you lived down here until last fall, and... well... my mom never talked about you guys. She just seemed sad if I asked about her family." Tears started showing in the young woman's eyes.

Eleanor covered Josie's hand with her own, patting it lightly. "It's alright dear. A lot of time has passed, that is very true." She fingered the wrinkles on her forehead before continuing. "But things are different now. So much has changed since I last spoke to your mother but I'm so glad, truly, truly glad that you found me."

Josie laughed. "Well, you weren't easy to track down. I had to go to nearly every Catholic church in Omaha and ask for you by name to whoever would listen to me before someone finally agreed to help."

"Who was it?"

"Alice was her name."

Eleanor laughed. "Oh Alice. She always was a sucker for a little gossip."

"Fortunately for us, I guess."

"Yes. It was fortunate." The elder woman looked sad for a moment, scanning Josie's face and hair, taking it all in. "All these years I've wondered if I would ever meet my grandchild."

"So, you didn't even know where we were?"

The elder shook her head. "No. And I didn't know if you were a boy or a girl to be honest."

A wide-eyed Josie just stared at the elder woman as a fresh cup of coffee was set before her.

"Unfortunately my husband, your grandfather, as it were, made it very clear to me and our two sons that Claire was no longer a part of our family and we were not to speak to her, or of her, ever again. He changed our phone number and we moved, and even switched churches, to make sure she didn't come knocking on the door." She blew across the top of her cup, cooling the black liquid before gingerly taking a sip.

"He doesn't sound very nice."

She shrugged. "Well, I won't speak ill of the dead, God rest his soul, but he was doing what he thought was best at the time. What was in line with his beliefs and values."

"Do you know that my mom wrote to you?" Josie gushed, unable to contain herself. "I have the letters. They're marked 'return to sender.'"

Sadness flashed across Eleanor's face before it was replaced with a gentle smile. "Thank you for telling me that, Josie. It makes me truly happy to know my daughter reached out to us. I didn't know about the letters, obviously, but would love to read them sometime if you're willing to share them with me."

Josie's face lit up. "Of course I will." Then reality hit her as she continued, more solemn this time. "But they're probably going to make you sad. Or mad even."

Eleanor leaned her head to the side, contemplating her response. "It's alright dear. Time changes people. God changes people. Sometimes we need to spend a little time apart so we can appreciate each other the way we ought to."

The two women ordered vanilla milkshakes from the peppy waitress, laughing at the fact that vanilla ice cream was their favorite, although boring to most people.

"How is your mother doing?" Eleanor asked, masking her eagerness behind a sip of coffee.

Josie sighed. "She's okay. I think." She gave Eleanor an exasperated look. "I don't really talk to her much."

"Oh?" said Eleanor.

Claire could tell she had a hundred questions to ask Josie but refrained, as any proper woman would do.

"It's a long story. Maybe I'll tell you some other time."

The older woman nodded.

"How did your husband die? Er, um, my grandpa." Josie said, looking desperate to change the subject.

Eleanor cleared her throat. "Lung cancer. It took him pretty quick about three years ago."

Claire gasped, cupping her hand over her mouth at the announcement. As mean as he was, he was still her father and the loss hit her hard.

"Oh, that's sad. I'm sorry," said Josie

"Thank you. But death is part of life. Everything has its time and season."

"It's too bad he couldn't meet me though, or see my mom again. Maybe they could have forgiven each other."

With a look of compassion, Eleanor leaned forward and spoke softly. "Truth be told dear, I think he regretted disowning her but he would never admit it. He was never the same after she left. He was sad and never raised his voice again, not even when one of our sons ran the car into the garage door. He did tell me, before he passed on, that he was sorry. He didn't say for what, but I know that what happened between him and Claire was the only thing he never confessed out loud to anyone."

CHAPTER 32

The In-between Place

"Oh daddy." Claire sobbed, dropping to her knees. Twenty years of pain rushed through her in a split second. Rocking back and forth she let the anger out with groans of pain. Her heart physically hurt as though the pus and infection of an open wound was being scraped off; discarded forever.

Several minutes later Claire composed herself enough to realize they were back on the riverbank. Jacob was by her side, his arm around her, head resting on her shoulder.

"Whoa! Wait. Where'd they go? I wanna go back to them, Jacob." She pleaded, looking around for the two women and knowing full well she wouldn't see them there. "Please Jacob? Can we please go back?"

"No. We can't." he said softly.

"But..." She dropped her head into her hands. "I don't understand. Why, if Josie found her, didn't I know about it? Did she tell me in one of her letters?"

Jacob shook his head side-to-side.

"So she intentionally hid that from me?" No anger this time; only sadness. "I don't understand."

"Sometimes God doesn't reveal things to us until we're ready for them," he said.

"But wouldn't it have been a good thing for me to see my mom and brothers again?" she whined. "Or try to make amends with my father before he died?"

He shrugged. "But what relationship is more important? You and your family? Or your relationship with God?"

"Um..." was all she managed.

"God doesn't make mistakes and His timing is always perfect. Josie needed family around her; Alan's family *and* your family. That's who God used to help in *her* healing process. But God's plan for your healing is different."

Claire had a lightbulb moment at the revelation. A surge of confidence flooded her knowing that God had taken care of her daughter, with not one but two grandmas, a grandpa, two uncles, Nick and a loving church family all these years. She also had a counselor and numerous friends who supported her healing process and in doing so, Josie had built a relationship with God, an others-centered career and a bridge toward restoration between Claire and her family.

"Oh. Yea. I get that now. Thanks." She flicked at the grass with her fingers, in awe of the revelation she'd just been given. So many years of needless worry when the whole time God did have Josie in His hands, caring for her through others and healing her from the inside out.

"You know, I was really angry with my dad and I know my anger has been a huge problem for a long time. I mean, I know the Bible says we can be angry but do not sin, but believe me, my anger wasn't justified." [1]

She took a deep breath and held it for a minute, slowing her heart rate. "Instead of admitting I was the one that had done wrong by getting pregnant I blamed my dad for kicking me out. I thought it was all his fault for being narrow minded and stringent and unloving and I've held that against him this entire time." She shook her head in self-reprimand.

"But it wasn't his fault at all. I was the one that had done wrong and he was just behaving based on how he believed. He was acting on his faith and morals and protecting his family. But me..." She paused to chuckle. After half a lifetime of projecting her faults onto others it seemed the only response. "I started this whole thing by my own sinful actions. Holding a grudge against him for all these years only tore me apart more and made me angry at God too, thinking that He's the one that gave me such mean parents and such bad luck with Alan dying and all that."

To even say this out loud is dumb. How could I have been so blind all these years?

"God reveals..." Jacob began.

She waved her hand at him, "Yea, yea, I know. When we're ready."

Exhaling strongly she stared at her hands, her shoulders drooping. "I see it now." *Oh daddy. I feel so bad about what I accused you of and what I thought about you. I'm so sorry.*

"I just wish I could have apologized to my dad before he died. I mean, really, honestly apologized and told him that I understand why he did what he did. I understand it now cuz I did the same thing with Josie." Her voice cracked as a sob escaped. "I acted on my beliefs and selfishness with the abortion. I thought what I was doing was okay, even good for her, but it wasn't."[2]

Wiping tears from her face, she continued. "Long term, it's not okay to act on a whim and speak rashly. I should have, and my dad probably should have too, consulted God first; prayed about it, and maybe sought counsel from other believers too, before making such a brutal decision."

She looked sadly at Jacob. "Like father, like daughter, huh?"

He shrugged, his innocence obvious.

"Or generational curses? A personality line so stubborn it refuses to listen to logic even at the expense of family."

"Sounds like he was sad about it though. I mean, from what your mom said about him."

Claire could only nod, her emotions getting the best of her and she paused to catch her breath.

"He had his own journey with God, just like you have yours." Jacob said. "Forgiveness is between a person and the Creator and it sounds like he made peace with it before passing on. Either way, it's God's deal, not yours. You can't change the past but you can have hope for the future cuz God says He's got a plan to prosper you.[3] Besides that, He uses situations like those between you, your dad and Josie, to further His kingdom and help others who are in need. It's all about service and surrender to Him and *His* plans, not our own, cuz His plans are always better for us."

"But why let bad things happen at all? To anyone? I mean, me getting pregnant was my fault. I totally accept responsibility for that one. But the rape wasn't Josie's fault and that's what started this mess."

"Sometimes what we see as negative events are actually part of God's ultimate plan for our lives and they define our purpose. Like with Josie. Her situation didn't happen to her until it passed through God's hands, through His wisdom and His knowledge of her future. And then He used that to teach her compassion, patience and grace, qualities she now uses to help others."

"But she suffered so much because of that man who traumatized her, and then by me…" she put her head in her hands breathing deeply to prevent more tears from coming.

"Suffering is a necessary part of a Christian's life and is part of living in this broken world. You see, we will one day share in Christ's glory and if we are to do that, then we also need to share in His suffering.[4] He had to endure many trials and temptations in His earthly life, even rejection and mocking, loneliness and pain, and so must we sometimes."

"Suffering," she pondered. "I feel like I've been suffering. For many years."

"And God is using that, He's been using all of this, to draw you close to Him, Claire. He wants to shape you, mold you and prepare you for your future. He has big plans for you, but you need to turn to Him so you can keep moving forward in your journey. You see, none of this can be done without Him. Just like He helped Josie, He also wants to help you."

"Oh boy. I don't know about that Jacob. I think I'm too far gone. I've lied and sinned so deeply. I mean… the abortion." She whispered the word as if saying it too loudly would cause her throat to swell shut.

"Do you know about Saul, the same guy that was later called Paul?"

Claire nodded. "Yea. Didn't he hunt down and kill Christians?"

"He did. He put them in prison and killed them, lots of them, for believing in Jesus. A pretty terrible guy at the time."[5]

Claire looked at him, anticipating the ending of his story.

"But then Saul met Jesus and the moment he did, he realized that the very one he hated was the one that he needed most. And Jesus was there, pursuing Saul, calling him toward the truth. Then Jesus transformed Saul's mind and heart and took one of the meanest people and turned him into a great missionary!"

Goosebumps covered Claire's arms.

"Then Saul was the one that was hated. People wanted to kill *him*, and they tried to, because they didn't believe he could go from killing Christians to being a believer in Jesus and preaching about Him as the Savior."

"Yea, I'm sure that was a big shock to everyone to see such a drastic change in his behavior. They were probably pretty confused about what happened."[6]

"But just like David, God saw his heart and knew his potential. God had a divine plan for his life and knew how to transform him from a murderer to a missionary. He knew how to fill him with new, God-pleasing passion and basically make him into a new person. I mean, not on the outside you know, cuz he still looked the same and everything." The boy smiled sheepishly.

Claire chuckled. "Yea, I know what you mean." It felt good to break the tension with humor and she found herself appreciating his.

"We can't see our whole life, but God can." Jacob continued. "He can have us going one direction, but in the blink of an eye, or a few minutes of meeting Jesus on that road like Saul did, everything can change!" His smile was broad and genuine. "Isn't that encouraging?"

Claire laughed, "It is." She looked at the young boy, grateful for his wisdom and encouragement and couldn't help but wonder how he would have been all grown up or what occupation he would have had as a man.

"Hey do you know the story about the blind man that Jesus healed?" he interjected.

"Um, kinda. My memory is a bit foggy."

"So Jesus saw a man who had been born blind and His disciples assumed that either the man or the man's parents had sinned and that's why he was born blind. But Jesus told them that it happened so that the works of God might be displayed through his healing. Cuz Jesus healed him, you know."[7]

"Yep, I remember that part."

"So it's just like we talked about. His whole life this guy was blind and probably struggled to do everything and missed out on so much joy from not being able to see, but God had a higher purpose for the man's suffering. It was so Jesus, at the perfect time, could perform a miracle and heal him in front of lots of witnesses, and then God got the glory!" The boy's excitement delighted her. "It was all to show of God's greatness and power. Do you get it?"

"Yea," Claire said. "I see that it's not about us, necessarily, it's about God and His purpose for our life and how He reveals Himself through us and our circumstances."

"Yep. And just the same, God has used Josie's suffering to bring her closer to Him and to fulfill her purpose. Ultimately to further His kingdom."

"Okay, so I understand that, but couldn't He teach Josie her lessons on compassion and helping others in a different way? I mean, maybe just give her a strong desire to help others and maybe an internship at a rape counseling center or something? You know, without the rape itself being involved? Couldn't there have been another way to get her into her career without destroying her innocence?"

"Yes, perhaps. But if God always intervened to save us from pain, then many people would only serve Him to gain that benefit. They wouldn't serve Him out of love and faithfulness, but out of selfishness."

She nodded in understanding. "Oh. That makes sense."

"Serving God should be a relationship of love and willing submission to His calling; a desire to serve the one who created us, not an obligation or just a desire to protect us from being hurt or experiencing pain."

Her breathing paused for a moment, processing his use of the word 'desire'. *I've desired to look good no matter how I felt, to be on time everywhere I went and to attend church regularly, but I've never felt the desire to truly get to know Christ. Adopting the heart of God as my own was never on my list of priorities.*

"And you know, those trials and the pain might be necessary to keep us faithful, or humble before God and His power. It's easy to drift away from God and become arrogant when everything is going our way."

Jacob said.

"Yea, that's true." said Claire. "I have experienced that before, back when I was in high school, living at home, just loving life with no hassles or problems." Her gaze drifted to the tree tops as she recalled how her mother did most everything for her and her younger brothers, letting Claire do as she wished for the most part. Not exactly the best choice on the part of her mom, given that Claire started hanging out with the wrong friends, ending up in trouble of her own due to a mostly hands-off mother and almost always absent father.

"I was in a godly home; we went to church all the time. But I didn't know God. I didn't have a relationship with Him." She shook her head in frustration, knowing her whole church-based young life had been in vain. "Actually I still don't think I do. Not a *real* relationship. The more I think about it, actually, I'm pretty sure it's all surface and fake."

Her voice was barely audible; her breath barely detectable as she comprehended the many poor decisions she'd made thus far in her life.

"Claire. Take a breath, it's okay. God doesn't give up on us. We may give up on ourselves, but He never tires of pursuing us." He rubbed her back with his small hand until she shuddered in a ragged breath. "God is using your own pain to make you see things more clearly, to really understand what's happened in your life and to bring healing to you."

"So I'm not hopeless?"

He giggled. "Well, there's some rough edges around you, but God is still doing good work through you, even though you get in your own way most times."

She laughed. "Yea. I do."

"Most everyone does," he said matter of factly. "They get so busy trying to fix everything themselves or control their lives, and forget that they're not in charge. God is. He created us so He has the ultimate say-so in our lives, we just have to surrender our lives to Him and trust Him to guide us."

"So..." She began, letting out an exasperated breath. "That's a tough one. Surrender."

The boy closed his eyes and turned his face toward the sky for a few moments, pausing in reverence to the Creator, before responding. "We are all born into sin, through Adam and Eve's original sin in the garden of Eden, and are sinful people by nature. It's just natural for us to be ungodly and that's why we need Jesus, cuz He redeemed us and died in our place. He was sin for us and died so that we could live, eternally."

"Yep, I get that."

"So when we're old enough to make decisions we make a choice to either continue to follow our sinful nature, which usually leads to bad stuff happening to us, or follow God. If we follow God, we choose to surrender our lives to Him and let Him lead us. God promises us that when we seek Him we will find Him [8] and says that His plans for our lives are better than our own plans. So we know it's gonna be good! Way better than we could even imagine!"

Jacob's excitement was contagious and Claire couldn't help but smile at him.

"It's difficult, you know," Claire explained. "Giving up control." Her smile had faded and seriousness returned again to her brow. "Especially as a single parent I felt like I had to have it all figured out. I was in charge of everything. Every decision, every mistake, every dollar made was up to me. I had to stay organized and productive and positive so that Josie wouldn't know how much I was struggling." She fumbled with another rock and tossed it into the river.

"The thought of surrendering to God during those years was unthinkable. I just didn't know if I could trust Him to take care of us the way I could."

She looked at the young boy's peaceful face. "Seems pretty silly, huh? To think I could do a better job than God?"

Even saying the words aloud made Claire cringe. How foolish was she and how much better could their lives have been if she'd drawn close to God twenty-five years ago instead of trying to do it all herself. She knew that God created the land and sea, the sky, sun and moon, all the animals and humans. He put the stars in the heavens, parted the Red Sea, brought the dead back to life and cast out demons, and she didn't trust Him to take care of her and Josie?

"God longs for a relationship with you. The Bible says that He wants to be in our hearts just like He wanted to be in Saul's heart. He stands at the door and knocks.[9] Just like this." Jacob hopped up on his feet and ran to the nearest tree, knocking on the ragged bark with his knuckles.

"*Knock knock,*" he said, peeking his head around the tree and smiling broadly at her. "Can I come in?"

Claire's eyes instantly filled with tears and before she could stop herself she stood up and hugged him tightly to her chest, sobbing into his dark hair.

Oh sweet Jacob. I adore you.

CHAPTER 33

Claire had drifted to sleep, something she didn't think was possible in this place. In her slumber she was walking through a concrete maze with walls so high they nearly blocked out the sunlight, when she came upon a large rock in the middle of the path. Compelled to stop, she noticed a small tree growing from a fissure. A green sprout of life in this otherwise desolate place. Two tiny leaves had emerged from the twig, stretching toward the distant sunlight, knowing that was the source of their life.

Stirring awake, Claire shifted her weight and sat up next to Jacob.

They were atop the river bottom hills, brome grass up to her shoulders, taking in the vast view before them. She swore they could see for a hundred miles in every direction from this vantage point, but what held her attention now were the details. Gone was the sparkling, shimmering vibrance that defined the in-between place. Instead the hues and textures of her normal world had returned.

She could see the roads, the rows of corn and soybeans growing in the fields nearby; the farm yards, windmills and barns. The country church was across the valley and cows roamed the pastures. Popcorn clouds promenaded freely across the sky making scattered shadows on the ground below. In and out of the clouds shadows popped the land and its features. The warm sun once again held its place in the sky.

Claire craned her neck slightly to glimpse the tops of the trees that marked her property, then let her gaze travel down to the valley again, following the river bends and turns until her eyes saw the bridge. She was relieved by the fact that her usual surroundings were back, but caught her breath at the sight of her car, visible now below the surface of the Jim River.

"I don't understand this, Jacob." her voice wavered slightly, "Am I dead now? Or what's going on with my car down there?" If she were alive it would be dark outside and she would either be in the car, escaping or laying on the river bank clawing her way out of the water's grip. And if she were dead, well then, this is probably the view she'd have. The aftermath. The view of what the world would have looked like the morning after she'd drown in the river, willingly stuck inside her car, floating in the murkiness all night.

"Am I dead?" she asked again, afraid of the answer.

"Maybe a better question to ask is if you're living?" His inquisitive eyes held hers. "You're alive, but are you really living? You've been angry for a really long time and you've missed so many blessings along the way by letting sin get the best of you."

The breeze picked at Claire's hair and she tucked it behind her ears.

"You should be living your life with joy and thankfulness. Every day! You should be with Josie, your family and your church, encouraging others and giving of your talents, not alone feeling guilty and scared."

"Here," he said, and handed her what appeared to be a greeting card tucked inside a crisp yellow envelope. "You need to open this."

On the front of the envelope was her own name and address with a postmark of July 1997. She glanced at the return name and read aloud.

"Josie and Nick Crowley." Giving Jacob a confused look, she ripped open the envelope and took out a card with the words *"Great News!"* printed on the front in bold letters. As she opened the card a photograph fell to her lap.

Staring back at her from the image was Josie, wavy hair pulled back at her temples, perfectly framing her oval face and pearl stud earrings. Her green eyes were bright with life and her smile stole the show. She was wearing a simple yet elegant white skirt that ended just above her knees and a lacy white blouse with cropped sleeves and pearl buttons on the front. *She looks like my mother. So classy and proper.*

Next to her was Nick, dressed in a navy blue suit, crisp white shirt and striped tie. His arm around Josie's waist and Claire thought there was never a man who looked more proud.

Claire's eyes went back to Josie's left hand, resting on Nick's chest, and noticed the ring. A simple gold band wrapped around her fourth finger.

She recognized Josie's handwriting in the card and read the words to

Jacob.

> *Mom. Guess what?! Nick and I celebrated our college graduations by going to the Courthouse and getting married! We've been talking about it for a couple years but wanted to finish school first. Please don't be mad that you weren't invited. No one else was there. Just us two. We plan to celebrate with you and the rest of the family when what we've been praying for comes to pass. No matter how long that might take.*
>
> *We miss you. We love you! Please note our new address on the envelope as we purchased our first home. It's only a one bedroom condo but it's got a great little balcony and is close to the Old Market. We love it!*
>
> *Hope to hear from you sometime! Until then, may the Lord bless and keep you. May His face shine upon you and be gracious to you. May He look upon you with favor and give you peace.[1] Josie*

Jacob turned to her when she was done, kneeling and taking her hands in his. "Remember when I told you that God had something for you?

"Yes," she said, forcing her mind to concentrate on what he was saying rather than wander to thoughts of Josie being a bride. *What were they praying for? And how long would they wait for an answer? Would they celebrate without her if it took too long?*

"It's another chance. He didn't send His Son to die for you so you could live in sadness and anxiety. Wake up, stand tall and move forward with the courage that Christ died to give you."

A flock of sparrows chatted as they rushed by, a black wave of perfectly synchronized winged bodies swooping through the air. Claire watched them as they fluttered down the hillside and across the river toward her cottage.

"Hear this. The Bible says that *He has torn us, that He may heal us; He has struck us down, and He will bind us up.*[2] Choosing the path to brokenness before God and others is difficult. It's scary and maybe embarrassing when past mistakes come out. But that path is always blessed by God because He told us that *His grace is sufficient for us and His power is made perfect in weakness.*[3] Jesus is waiting for you to respond to Him, and what He has for you will be marvelous!"

Hope shone in Claire's eyes for the first time in decades as the boy's words resonated deep in her soul. Tears of joy streamed down her face. She longed to return to her life and start over; with Josie and Nick as her son-in-law, her church, neighbors and herself. And reconnect with her mother and brothers. *Oh how I miss them.* The desire to live, and live in accordance with God's plan, was overwhelming and she felt she may burst with joy at the prospect of having another chance.

"It's time to go now," he said softly, standing and taking her hand in his to help her up..

Fear caught in her throat as she clenched his hand tightly. There was no time to process the marriage or being back in 'reality' or seeing her own car beneath the water.

"But... what about you?" Her voice faltered. Thinking about leaving him behind trumped all other thoughts for the moment.

"What about me?"

"You... um... will I ever see you again?" Her hands were trembling now as anxiety pricked at the back of her neck. *I did this to him. To myself and our family.*

He smiled broadly and nodded. "Eventually."

Claire shook her head vigorously, trying to shake the pain from her heart. Regret hung heavy around her neck, choking off her air supply. "But how do I go beyond this Jacob?" she whispered.

He leaned in to hug her. "You start by understanding that I forgive you. God's got this handled and He's going to work it out for your good and to glorify His kingdom."

"But how do I forgive myself for what I did to you?" She couldn't stop from crying openly.

"Talk to God about it. His grace and mercy are freely available for you and He will heal you. In here," he touched her head, "and in here," he said as he touched her heart.

She pulled him tighter against her chest. "I don't know how to say goodbye to you." She sobbed into his dark hair, not wanting to let him go, afraid of what leaving him would mean. "I'm so sorry Jacob. I'm so sorry I took you away from Josie and from our home."

He let her process the moment, squeezing her tightly and letting her enjoy holding him in her arms. "It's alright. I'm okay, and Josie's okay and you're gonna be okay too. Remember, God has a purpose for everything under Heaven,[4] and we're all a part of that purpose in one way or another."

She leaned back from him, gently touched his cheek before running her hands through his hair, trying to memorize him by touch. *My grandson.* "I love you Jacob."

"I love you too Grandma."

The reference made Claire smile as the purest form of happiness filled her heart. She clutched the photo of Josie and Nick close to her chest and brought her face close to Jacob's until their foreheads met. Her eyes involuntarily closed as incredible, unexplainable peace flooded over her mind and body. Warmth spread throughout her chest, then radiated into her arms and legs. A spine tingling sensation caused her body to jolt as if being shocked by an electrical circuit.

Then the pain hit.

CHAPTER 34

The James River – July 2005

Claire was gasping and wheezing, her lungs on fire with a pain she'd never experienced before. She couldn't breathe. Her chest was heavy and tight. Her body cold and wet and without obedience to her will to move her rigid limbs.

In the next instant coughing overtook her body like waves crashing onto an unsuspecting shore as she was rolled to her side by another's hands, emitting river water from her lungs and allowing room for precious air in its stead. Burning, intense and unpleasant, followed close behind, leaving her intently aware that she was very much alive.

Distant sirens could be heard above the river valley hills. Nearly as distant was a man's voice; muffled and deep. His words resonated in the recesses of her mind but his utterances made no sense. Her focus remained on her lungs and their desperate attempts for relief. *Was this hell? Is satan talking to me? Is he nice to new residents at first, before the torture starts? Fair enough.* She accepted her fate.

She felt her body being rolled to the side once again and this time a sharp pain shot through her arm as her weight pressed on it. More rough coughing and then vomiting. She tried to wipe her mouth but her arm wouldn't work. The muffled voice was there again, more clear. "It's okay".

What's okay? She certainly wasn't okay. The pain was nearly unbearable. The sharp stabs of twigs and rocks beneath her body became more evident as her mind started to clear. She writhed, so uncomfortable in every way possible; her left arm especially tender. Trying to push herself up with her right arm she moaned in agony.

"Hold on now." That man's voice again, very clear this time and more stern. "Lie still. You're hurt."

She could feel water dripping off his face onto hers as he leaned over her, one hand clamped around her left bicep, the other brushing her tangled wet hair off her face.

With each breath, labored against tender ribs, she inhaled more precious air until she felt sure enough of her ability to open her eyes for a peek at her surroundings, terrified to discover if she was amongst hellfire and brimstone.

The slit of vision allowed by her heavy eyelids revealed a dark haired man, bearded with broad shoulders covered with a plaid shirt, hovering above her; his eyes intent on scanning the distant hills rather than her own. A glinted reflection of moonlight around his neck caught her eye. A necklace. *The cross.*

Her eyes closed involuntarily as another wave of pain swept over her. The sirens were louder now and she tried to clear her head about where she had been.

The boy was real. He was there with her, that she knew without a doubt. But how? And where was he now? *Oh Jacob.* Her heart ached for the things he had revealed to her; the things he had shown her. *The truth.* Her regret hurt deeply. Too deep to hold onto any longer. She longed to get to Josie and seek forgiveness.

She tried to sit up again but the man held her down.

"Just a few more minutes." The man said, his deep voice resonating in the cool midnight air. "You're gonna be okay. The ambulance isn't that far away."

His reassurances that she'd be okay fell on deaf ears. Her body might be okay, but her soul? Now that her lungs were functioning again, the sobs came. And they were unstoppable. Despite the intense pain in her ribcage, she let them roll through her body, grieving for all the years she'd lost with Josie, the pain she'd caused her beloved daughter, the blessings she'd missed out on because of her pride and ignorance. *And Jacob. That sweet boy. What have I done?*

"Forgive me," she moaned, "Oh Jesus, please forgive me."

The sirens got louder as the man's hands tenderly held her.

"I killed him, God. Oh…" She couldn't breathe for a moment as the psychological pain overtook her entire body and her body began to shake violently. "I killed my grandson. Oh Lord… Jesus… Please forgive me."

Pain more intense than anything physical she'd experienced in her life filled her body, causing her to gasp for air. "I'm so sorry. I was so wrong. Please forgive me."

CHAPTER 35

Mercy Hospital, Yankton, South Dakota – July 2005

Hushed whispers could be heard hovering about in the still air. The soft *beep beep beep* of a machine kept perfect rhythm and more distantly a woman's matter-of-fact voice on an intercom paged doctor so-and-so.

Claire forced her eyes open, although sleep felt more enticing and certainly would have been a more comfortable place to stay. A blonde haired nurse in yellow scrubs and a doctor in a traditional white coat stood near the door to her hospital room, identical looks on their serious faces, as they flipped through papers attached to a clipboard. The nurse glanced up to see Claire's alertness and Claire recognized her as a co-worker, Margo, who'd been working at the hospital since before Claire started there nearly thirty-one years prior.

"Hey Claire." Margo walked toward the bed, a hitch in her step from years of walking the sterile white halls and lifting countless patients up off low-rise beds. "Welcome back. Glad to see you're with us again." She smiled gingerly and grasped Claire's hand with one of hers while the other caressed Claire's hair off her forehead. "You had us a bit worried hun."

Margo's lips were pursed, her eyes slanted, and Claire knew well enough that something was amiss. Two women don't work together for over thirty years without getting to know the 'shows' of concern, doubt or worry as they appear across the other's face.

Doctor Roger Meens stood beside Margo smiling gently, as was his consistent bedside manner despite the seriousness, or lack thereof, of any given situation while he was on shift. His white hair stood out starkly against his tanned skin; his blue eyes reflected the daylight coming in from the window. Claire recalled he and his wife had just returned a couple days ago from a three week vacation in Arizona to see their two children and five grandchildren. Obviously he'd gotten in a lot of golf, as was his desire per his confiding in Claire during a coffee-break conversation prior to their departure.

Dr. Meens was a friend of Claire's as his daughter, Gina, had babysat Josie years ago. There were times when their normal babysitter, an elderly neighbor lady, was feeling ill, so she'd take Josie to Yankton with her, drop her off at the doctor's home for Gina to watch for the entirety of the night until Claire got off work at seven a.m. It had only happened a few times but Claire was eternally grateful to have their assistance. Now as he looked at her, like Margo, Claire could tell there was concern in his eyes and something negative behind his smile. Reading his facial expressions and body language was part of her job especially when cases were critical or death was imminent. After so many years together, the co-workers knew one another better than most spouses.

"Hi Roger." Claire squeaked out. Her throat was dry and Margo was ready with the water glass and straw. Drinking cautiously, she looked up at Dr. Meens as if to say "what's wrong with me?" with her eyes and furrowed brow.

"Claire," he started, "Good to see you awake. You've been out for nearly fourteen hours." He positioned himself at the edge of the bed as Margo went around the other side to adjust Claire's pillows. "We're going to sit you up a bit and see how that feels. You've got two fractured ribs from the chest compressions you received so you're going to be pretty sore for a while."

Margo started to raise the head of the bed, a couple inches at a time as Claire squirmed to stay as comfortable as possible. She was no wimp when it came to physical discomfort having been on her feet every night for twelve hour shifts for so many years, and she tried hard to keep her pain hidden now from those she most respected.

Wincing, she finally told Margo that was far enough and Dr. Meens nodded in approval at her determination and progress. "We put a dozen or so stitches into this gash on your left arm after we removed a few pieces of glass. It should heal up just fine though. Cut some muscle tissue but no tendons." He stated, indicating the wide white bandages wrapped around her left bicep. "Probably leave a decent scar but nothing too terrible."

Claire nodded her understanding then looked at him quizzically. "I can tell from your face that something else is going on." She managed a weak smile for him. "What is it?" Despite her exterior optimism, inside she was braced for the worst.

His face turned serious as he asked Margo to give them privacy. He wouldn't meet Claire's gaze as he turned back toward her. He kept his head down, looking at his hands clasped in his lap. He took a deep breath. Then another. Then cleared his throat a couple of times.

Claire felt panic arise in her own throat, afraid that perhaps the boy had been real and she'd hit him and killed him or something equally as horrible.

He spoke hesitantly at first. "The man that rescued you followed the ambulance to the hospital." His gaze met hers. "And he has sat in the waiting room for the past fourteen hours wanting to make sure you were okay."

Claire wondered why a perfect stranger would care so much as to do that but knew that wasn't the news that was causing her friend to look so worried.

"He gave his statement to the police last night and then I spoke to him this morning to get the details of your rescue and subsequent injuries so they could be documented properly." His brow furrowed deeply with concern, was it? Or something more dire?

"He told me something in confidence that is quite disturbing and before I talk to authorities about it myself, I wanted to get your side of the story." His eyes finally met and held hers with such intensity she thought for certain she'd have a heart attack right there in front of him.

"He told me that last night, right before the ambulance arrived, you called out to God and asked for forgiveness for killing your grandson."

Claire's breathing quickened and shame washed over her in red sheets, as tears filled her eyes.

"That's some serious stuff Claire. Can you please tell me what happened before I assume the absolute worst?" he said, his eyes wavering nervously between fear and tears.

His face was deceptive and she could tell, from years of experience, that this wasn't her friend talking to her, this was a mandatory reporter and his seriousness was demanding she speak quickly and explain thoroughly.

Muddled thoughts were whipping a hundred miles an hour through Claire's mind. The past twelve years of pain and guilt; the abortion; the distance between herself and Josie; the Jim River boy that showed her things she'd never known or had, herself, assumed the worst about. The knowledge of her dad's death and mother's love. It was all too overwhelming and she felt panic creeping into her throat. She closed her eyes, held her breath and prayed.

Father God, I need you. I need your strength. I need your peace. Please be with me now. In Jesus' name.

An overwhelming peace fell upon her as Jacob's words resounded in her head, "*Jesus said that He leaves us with his peace. Peace that we can't understand or explain.*"[1]

Hot tears spilled onto Claire's cheeks as she took Roger's hand in both of hers. As her friend and co-worker she knew he'd understand more than anyone else would.

"Josie was raped the night she graduated from high school." Claire's voice was raspy with emotion and fatigue. "She didn't tell me about it until about four weeks later, and only then because she was pregnant."

Roger's eyes softened and compassion spread across his face as he began to figure out where this story was leading.

"I didn't believe her story about her being raped and because of my pride and embarrassment at what that would mean for us in the church and community, and what that would do for Josie's future, I forced her to get an abortion."

The intense guilt and pain she expected to feel at speaking those words out loud for the first time ever didn't happen. Instead the peace stayed with her, persistent and strong. She could feel God's hand of comfort upon her and she knew He had forgiven her. She had confessed her worst sin last night on the banks of the James River and cried out in sincerity for forgiveness, and He had heard her. *He is faithful and just to forgive us.*[2] *Thank you God. Thank you!*

Roger stared sadly at Claire after she finished explaining herself and nodded his head as if he knew and understood the pressing circumstances that led her to do such a thing.

"Okay," he said.

"I had to come to terms with what I did and confess it to God and that's what last night was about," she said, squeezing his hand. "I can't really explain it all, Roger. I've just been in denial about it and living in shame for all these years, but it's okay now." She smiled broadly. "I've been set free."

Roger patted her arm. "While I don't condone what you did, it's not for me to judge, Claire. I wasn't in your shoes." His voice was sincere and soft. "As Christians we are to love and encourage, and so I will continue to do that and to pray for you, as I do for all my staff and friends, and give thanks that you have found redemption and peace." His misty eyes held compassion as he stood from the bed. "You get some rest. I'll check on..."

"I would really like to get out of here and find Josie." She started to remove the blanket from her legs and gasped in pain.

"Whoa! Come on now. You can't just jump out of bed and be on your way." Dr. Meens sounded more like a father than a doctor. "You're staying here at least another night and we'll see about releasing you tomorrow morning." He covered her legs back up and went around the bed to lower it back into a sleeping position. "*Maybe* release you tomorrow," he reiterated.

"But I need..."

"What you *need*... is to get some rest," He insisted, pointing a stern finger at her. "And I'll come back before my shift ends and check on you." He walked toward the door, turning back as he held the door knob. "Thank you, Claire, for trusting me enough to tell me the truth." Hesitating to clear his throat, he placed his hand over his heart before continuing. "I'm sorry you and Josie had to go through that painful experience. Please, *please* let me know if there's anything I can do to help you two."

Claire nodded, wiping her nose with a tissue.

"Oh, yeah. I nearly forgot. Clinton's still in the waiting room." Dr. Meens said, nodding toward the hallway.

"Who?"

"Clinton. The man who pulled you out of the river. Remember I told you that he's been here since last night when you were brought in."

She raised her eyebrows. *I sorta remember him saying that. I'm so tired.*

"He's asked to see you, if you're up for that."

Claire suddenly got butterflies in her stomach. "Well, the man did save me. The least I can do is say thank you."

She nodded to the doctor and the bearded man in the plaid shirt entered the room a short minute later, quietly closing the door behind him.

His dark hair was dry now, slightly wavy but cut short with a full beard covering his jawline. It framed a handsome face with strong features and chocolatey brown eyes that took in the sight before him in one sweeping gaze.

"Well, you're looking a lot better than you did last night." he chided, revealing a perfect smile.

Claire tried to laugh, noting his tired eyes. *He looks worse than I feel.* He probably hadn't slept much on the tiny couches in the waiting room. *What kind of man waits all night to make sure a stranger is okay?*

"I'm Clinton." he offered her his hand. "Not sure if you remember that from last night or not. You were pretty out of it."

"Claire, and no." taking his hand. "I didn't remember your name, just the plaid shirt, beard and necklace." She looked for it now, seeing its outline tucked under the collar of his dark blue undershirt.

Instinctively he touched it. "I wear it nearly every day. Not at work, but otherwise every day."

She looked at him curiously, intrigued by the man who pulled her from the river.

"Farmer and part time EMT." He answered her unspoken question. "I help out with the Tabor County ambulance service."

"No kidding? Wow! How convenient then that you were the one to pull me from the river."

"Yea, weird story there." He paused to scratch his head. "I was on my way home from my folks' place up by Clayton and got a flat tire along the way. Which isn't odd by any means, I guess, except that it delayed my trip home by thirty minutes or so. If that hadn't happened I wouldn't have seen your car go off the bridge." He placed his hands on his hips, looking thoughtfully at her.

"God?" She whispered.

"Yea, I reckon it was."

CHAPTER 36

Distant voices brought Claire's awareness to a more conscious level. A woman's. A man's. *Is that Dr. Meens?* Then the door opened and the excitement burst in.

Through half-open eyes Claire saw Josie push past the doctor and rush toward the bed.

"She's resting Josie." The doctor insisted to deaf ears.

"Mom!" She had her hands all over Claire's face and arms, as a mother would check her child for injuries after falling off a bike. "Mom, are you okay? Oh my gosh. I got here as fast as I could. You look hurt. Are you hurt?"

Her face was so concerned that Claire couldn't help but smile inside. "Hi honey," she said groggily, her nap wearing off in layers.

Josie talked with her hands and right now they were flailing about like a fledgling falling from a nest. "They said you'd been in a car accident but they didn't give me any details. And then I heard on the radio that a local woman had run her car off the Jim River bridge and I thought maybe it was you but the hospital wouldn't tell me anything on the phone. All they said was that you were here... and, and unconscious and to get here as quickly as I could and..."

"Stop." Claire said softly, a look of absolute love in her eyes as she touched her beautiful daughter's face with her hand. "Breathe, Josie." She found humor in her daughter's ramblings, wondering if the woman took even one breath during the waterfall of words that just fell from her mouth.

"Huh?" Josie startled back to reality.

"Stop talking. I have something to say to you and it can't wait." Her ribs hurt like no one's business but the insistence of the Holy Spirit to cleanse her soul was stronger.

She motioned for Josie to sit next to her on the bed. "Yes, I crashed my car off the bridge last night." Josie gasped at the thought. "But I'm okay. A few fractured ribs, cuts and scrapes, but nothing to be concerned about." Her hand held Josie's.

"What made you crash? Were you...?"

Claire smiled and placed a finger over Josie's lips to prevent her from continuing.

"I'll tell you everything later but right now I need to apologize." The grogginess from her nap had fully worn off but now emotion stuck in her throat, making speech difficult. "I am so very, very sorry for what I forced you into all those years ago. I apologize for the pain I caused you; for the tension between us; for ignoring your letters and calls; and for all the lost years." She paused to clear her eyes of the tears that hid her amazing child from view.

"I was prideful and arrogant and just plain mean. I was confused and depressed and scared and embarrassed and more afraid of what everyone would think about you and I than I was about what God would think."

Sobs threatened to end her speech and she paused to take several deep breaths. "Here. Can you press that little button and get this bed adjusted so I can sit up?"

The head of the bed began to rise and Claire grimaced in pain, secretly glad for the distraction as it helped her regain her composure.

"I did a terrible thing by making you have an abortion and I ask your forgiveness, honey." Her bottom lip quivered as fresh tears started to fall.

The lifted burden from Josie's shoulders was poignantly obvious as the worry lines on her forehead dissipated, her shoulders and neck relaxed, and the tears welled up in her own eyes. She reached out to wipe the tears from her mother's cheeks. "Oh... I forgave you a long time ago Momma."

Claire's shoulders slumped forward and she started to sob as Josie came forward, pulling her close, careful to avoid the bandages on her mother's left arm.

"I've been praying for you every day since then," Josie said. "Asking the Lord for His work to be done in you so you would find healing and forgiveness in Him. That you would know His peace in your heart."

Claire nodded her head into Josie's shoulder, relishing the contact from the one person she'd longed for for so many years. She sat back and held Josie at arm's length.

"Something happened during my car accident," she explained, clearing her throat. "I finally saw the truth. God opened my eyes and I saw everything for what it was from back when you were a kid up until now. I saw it all so clearly." She managed a smile and gave up on wiping the tears away. She let them fall. They were cleansing her soul and making their relationship clean again.

"My apologies are so many years too late, but with God's grace we can start again, right here, and move forward." Josie nodded her head in agreement, her smile broad across her tear streaked face.

"Josie, I'm sorry I didn't believe you when you told me you were raped. I'm sorry I didn't slow down long enough to really get to know you when you were in middle school and high school. I was so worried about keeping appearances up and making money that I neglected you and your needs. I should have spent more time with you and then I would have known how amazing you were. I would have known you would never lie to me." The words gushed out of her like doves escaping from a cage.

"Breathe, Mom." Josie chuckled, using her mother's previous words against her.

Claire smiled and sucked air into her lungs, wincing in pain despite her shallow breaths.

"God is gracious and merciful, and His Spirit helps us behave that way too." Josie said, her green eyes full of compassion. "All is forgiven, Mom. It truly is. I'm okay and I've been okay for a very long time." She squeezed her mother's hand tightly. "Now it's my hope that we can focus on *your* healing so we can start celebrating life again like we used to."

Claire's peace was evident on her face, her eyes lit up with anticipation of what the coming years would bring. "We *will* celebrate. Every day we will celebrate life and second chances." She clutched at her heart, certain she'd have a heart attack from all the happiness spilling out of her.

"And we can celebrate our first life event, *together*, right now." Josie announced.

Claire gave her a quizzical look.

"I assume you haven't read the letters I've been sending you?"

The look of shame on Claire's face said it all. "I'm so sorry honey. I..."

"It's okay Mom. I figured you weren't, otherwise you certainly would have called me as soon as you got the latest one." She raised her eyebrows, indicating some very big news had been announced in it.

"Oh yea?" said Claire, her curiosity piqued.

Josie stood and pulled her t-shirt tight across her abdomen, revealing a slight bump.

"We're having a baby!" she announced, pride and joy emanating from her face.

Claire stared at the evidence of a new life growing inside her daughter and caught her breath. She heard the Holy Spirit say to her, "*I make all things new*".

CHAPTER 37

Claire's Home - September 2005

Yellow and orange leaves clung to the branches of Claire's trees with the little strength they had left for the season. A slight breeze could have caused them to make the short flight to the ground, but today there was none, just perfect stillness as the early fall sun hung overhead.

"This is my favorite time of year," said Nick, bringing yet another armload of folding chairs out of the trailer and setting them around round tables which had been spaced out on the lawn.

"Mine too," said Claire, right beside him with floral centerpieces composed of fresh yellow roses, white spider mums, orange alstroemeria and red Gerber daisies. Their color scheme perfectly complemented the display hovering above them in the tree canopy. "The smell of fall is so wonderful."

A loud cackling came from the brooder house, causing both Nick and Claire to pause in place to see what the fuss was about.

"Probably fighting over who's the prettiest." Nick offered, getting a laugh out of his mother-in-law. "It's good to hear chickens out here again, Claire. I remember how much fun they were to watch when Josie and I were in high school."

"Fun to watch? Or chase around with your bicycles?" she joked, recalling what the two youngsters had often done with their flock of egg layers.

A dark red Ford pickup pulled into the driveway, making its way past the weeping willow tree and parking on the south side of the garage.

"Is that Clint?" said Nick.

The big smile on Claire's face was all the proof he needed.

"Looks like that's his normal parking spot, huh?" he teased as she practically skipped toward the pickup, her dark green dress kicking up behind her.

"Keep unloading chairs young man." She dismissed Nick with a wave of her hand.

The screen door opened then closed with its predicted *bang*, a feature Claire had purposefully insisted on as it reminded her of her childhood home's back screen door. Any time she or her brothers would race outside to play, the final child would let the door slam behind them, to the chagrin of their mother, but it was a memory lodged into Claire's mind as one of the most wonderful sounds she'd ever known.

Josie emerged from the house, her belly showing well beneath her rust colored sundress.

"You gonna be warm enough in that, Honey?" said Nick.

"It's nearly seventy-five degrees," she chided her husband.

"Okay, okay." He laughed and pretended to protect himself from the verbal darts she was throwing. "I'm just trying to protect my investment."

"Oh stop it, you silly man." On tip-toe she kissed him soundly before turning to see her mother walking toward them, hand-in-hand with Clinton. "Aww, they look so happy."

Before greetings could be exchanged, the loud honking of two car horns blasted at them from the road.

Claire clapped with delight. "That's Mom, Shawn and Luke."

A dark gray Suburban pulled up alongside a white Honda and five kids between the ages of nine and eighteen spilled out of both back seats.

"Auntie Claire!" the youngest two yelled, rushing forward and throwing themselves into her open arms.

"Hello Broccoli Head and Booger," she said, kissing them on the cheeks. They giggled with delight at her silly nicknames and kissed her back before rushing off toward the brooder house.

"Hey! Don't throw rocks at the chickens like you did last time!" Claire yelled to their retreating backs. "Goofy kids." She loved the sound of the children's' laughter echoing through the yard and followed them with her eyes, half wishing she could join their adventures.

The remaining teenage kids greeted her with less flamboyance, hugging her and Josie in turn and shaking hands with the two men.

"Hello Mother." Claire hugged her mother for a long minute. "It's been so long."

Eleanor laughed and squeezed Claire's shoulders, looking wistful. "Two weeks certainly seems like a long time, doesn't it?" The women gazed into each other's eyes and smiled.

Claire hadn't yet returned to work since the car accident nearly three months prior. Dr. Meens insisted the cut to her left arm be healed completely so as not to cause further damage by Claire lifting patients at the hospital. "Besides that, you haven't used any vacation days in nearly eight years. I'll see you back here in November", he had told her sternly, knowing she had a lot of catching up to do with her daughter and family during the recovery.

The first order of business, once Claire's ribs had healed and she was well enough to travel, was to arrange to meet with her mother and brothers in Omaha. She had discovered they both lived near their mother, had gotten married and each had children of their own. Shawn, the younger, had two and Luke, the elder, had three.

Josie had gone with her and the reunion was just as Claire imagined it would be. There were the apologies from Claire to Eleanor for her rancid behavior and ignorance, the disbelief at how tall and handsome her brothers had become, and endless hugs and tears of joy. Meeting her nieces and nephews was even more exciting and Claire tried desperately to remember all of their names that first day, finally giving up and coming up with creative nicknames for the five based on their looks and behavior.

Since that first reunion, Claire, with Clinton oftentimes by her side, split her time between Omaha and her acreage where her brothers would visit on weekends, bringing their mother, the wives and children with them every time. Everyone pitched in to help her get the brooder house repaired and a handful of chickens settled in. The tire swing was replaced with a sturdier seat and new rope and a tree fort was built four feet off the ground between three large trees in the grove, its raw wood walls painted with whatever random leftover buckets of paint Claire could dig out of her garage. Dark green, white, light blue, beige and mauve with a hinged front door that squeaked loudly when opened.

"Auntie Claire?" Adele, a.k.a. 'Booger', had asked her one day. "Can we put a lock on the door so no one breaks in and steals nothin'?"

Claire laughed at the notion given the 'things someone might steal' were empty tin cans, several half-crushed pop cans, an empty jar of pickles with a missing lid and some mismatched dishes Claire relinquished from her kitchen. Oh yes, and several homemade mud pies sitting on a crooked shelf.

"Um, of course you can," she'd replied. "But you do remember that the back of the tree fort is wide open. Right?"

Adele didn't seem to mind that there was no back wall to the tree fort, just a piece of old stair railing to serve as their balcony, insisting that no one would think about looking back there once they saw the lock on the front door.

The family talked for hours on end when they were together, Claire, her brothers and their mother. They obsessed over Eleanor's old photo albums, recalling the fun they had together as children, while constantly being interrupted by the nieces and nephews' stories of school, friends, sporting events and *watch what I can do, Auntie Claire* requests. It was overwhelming and exhilarating all at the same time and Claire wouldn't have had it any other way.

This day, this warm October day, was the long-awaited celebration of Josie and Nick's marriage, eight years prior. The entire church congregation was invited, their family and neighbors, several of the young couple's friends from high school, Claire's co-workers and of course Alan's parents, of whom Claire had seen twice since the accident.

Theirs was a stoic and heartwarming reunion during which time the couple insisted Claire had nothing to apologize for. *"You let by-gones be by-gones and trust the Lord's plan. Let's just pick up where we left off and treasure every day we have with each other and Josie too,"* her father-in-law stated. *"You are our daughter and we love you. Always have."* And that was that. They spent the day catching up on the goings-on of the past many years since they'd last visited and vowed to be involved with each other's lives regularly going forward.

Claire's new appreciation for life was evident all around her, from the repairs done to the acreage and outbuildings, to the way she carried herself and spoke. Usually smiling with gratitude and joy that came from an endless well filled with living water by her Savior.

CHAPTER 38

Twilight saw Claire's yard filled with guests, some sitting around the tables visiting and nibbling at wedding cake, and others milling about on the lawn and under the trees, enjoying the gorgeous evening and slowly emerging stars. In all, Claire figured about one hundred twenty people were there to honor and celebrate the marriage and the upcoming birth of her grand-baby.

Alan's parents had arrived early as did Dr. Meens, insisting he, his wife and daughter Gina attend to witness God's graciousness at work.

"Claire?" a soft voice said beside her, causing Claire to turn.

"Rachel! Hi!" She gave the woman a big hug. "I'm so glad you're here. Did you bring the family?" Not even the thought of the woman's many, unruly children running rampant through her yard, or house, gave pause to Claire.

"Um, well, yes we did." The woman admitted hesitantly, bracing for a lecture on the do's and don'ts of Claire's home. "Is that okay? I mean, they were invited, right?"

Claire smiled broadly even as she heard the chickens in an uproar once again and envisioned Rachel's children chasing them with sticks. "Yes of course they were invited and I'm glad you're here. I've been meaning to talk to you sooner but with your family gone this summer, I..."

"Yea, we were on our annual camping trip." The woman interjected, laughing. "Fourteen National Parks in eight weeks."

"That's wonderful," said Claire. "Kudos to you for making those family memories. Say, while I have your ear, I need to apologize for my behavior toward you over the years. I shamefully admit I've spoken badly about you behind your back and criticized you too and I deeply regret that. Will you forgive me?"

Rachel was speechless, wide-eyed, staring at Claire as though she'd seen a ghost.

"I'd like to renew our friendship and work together to figure out how to rearrange the church library so there's more room for books and maybe even a couple of lounge chairs so folks can sit and read." Claire continued.

Rachel nodded, snapping out of her stupor. "I'd really like that Claire and yes, of course, I do forgive you. Thank you for... well... for saying that to me. I appreciate it."

The clinking of a spoon on a champagne glass brought their attention to where Nick and Josie stood on the front steps of the house, their appearance similar to the wedding photo they'd sent to Claire so long ago, save for Josie's dress color and baby bump.

"Excuse me everyone. Please gather close by. My lovely wife has something she'd like to say." said Nick, putting his arm around Josie.

"Thank you for being here and helping us celebrate. We truly love seeing all of you here together and catching up with you has been a hoot." A *'yea buddy'* yell came from the back and Nick rolled his eyes, knowing it was their friend Chris, whom they hadn't seen for a couple of years.

"When we got married, Nick and I agreed that we would celebrate together, with *all* of our family in attendance, when God answered some very specific prayers." She looked at her mother, teary eyed, and smiled.

"And He has."

Clint put his arm around Claire's waist and kissed her temple knowing how much the reunion of family meant to her.

"It's been a long road but God is faithful and He's brought us together again and has blessed us with an upcoming baby too." Her hands wrapped around her belly and she turned side-ways, showing off the growing bump.

The guests broke out in loud applause and someone hollered for music and dancing.

"I'll take care of that," Clinton said to Claire, making his way toward the house where he and Shawn had already set up speakers in the open windows. As he passed by Eleanor he lightly grabbed her elbow.

"Excuse me Miss Ellie, may I have a moment of your time?" he said.

"Why yes, young man." She smiled at him. "What's on your mind?"

Clint glanced back at Claire to ensure she wasn't eavesdropping, then proceeded. "I would like your permission to ask your daughter to be my wife."

Eleanor gasped, then laughed, hugging him tightly. "Oh yes. Of course, of course. I give you my blessing and might add that I'm delighted beyond words to have you as my son-in-law." She pinched his cheek as though he were a child.

"Thank you ma'am."

"Does she know your intentions?" she said.

He shook his head and placed a finger over his mouth indicating to keep it secret.

EPILOGUE

December 2005

"Why is this elevator so slow?" Claire said under her breath, twisting the gold banded diamond on her left hand while she counted the seconds.

Finally the doors opened and, taking a sharp right turn, she nearly ran into Clinton who had arranged to meet her at the hospital.

"Room 304. I already asked the nurse," he said, taking her hand and leading her down the hallway past a sign that said "Maternity Ward".

"Thank you. I'm so excited I almost peed my pants on the way here." she said, laughing alongside him as they all but ran down the hallway.

A light knock brought a *"come in"* reply from Nick and the two guests entered the room.

Josie sat in bed, head propped up, looking like a million bucks and not like she'd just gone through labor.

"Hi sweetheart," Claire said, rushing forward and giving her daughter a kiss on the forehead. "How're you feeling?"

"I feel great, Mom." She beamed with happiness. "Two hours of pain is nothing compared to the joy of holding my baby."

"Two hours?!" Claire shrieked. "That's it?" Astounded, she looked at Clint while pointing a sharp finger at Josie. "I was in labor for sixteen hours with this girl."

Clint laughed. "Well, it was worth every second." Leaning forward to squeeze Josie's shoulder. "Congratulations kiddo," he said.

Nick approached Claire with a bundle in his arms. "Here you go, Grandma. I know you're anxious to meet your grandson."

"A boy?" said Claire, her heartbeat racing. At the moment she didn't even try to stop her mind from thinking about Jacob and how she could have held *him* in her arms all those years ago.

Eyes wide, she took the baby from Nick and pushed back the light green blanket to reveal the newborn's face. His eyes were closed in restful sleep and a mop of dark hair covered his head. Round cheeks, just like Josie had as an infant, made him look chunkier than he was.

A soft sigh escaped Claire's lips as Clint came up beside her, taking in his first view of the little man and caressing the feather soft hair.

"Wow," he said. "He's a handsome fella."

"He sure is," said Claire. "He's perfect." *And that hair!*

Too in awe to speak, Claire just stared at the boy. *My grandson. Oh how I love you darling. I will always protect you.*

"What's his name?" Clint asked, looking from Nick to Josie.

"Alan Jacob," announced Nick proudly.

Claire caught her breath. She hadn't told anyone about meeting Jacob at the Jim River. Although she and Josie now talked about everything under the sun, Claire never did tell her what happened the night of the accident, and Josie never questioned it. She knew God had intervened in her mother's life and changed her literally overnight, and she was grateful for that. And that was enough. She didn't need to know details.

"Alan?" Claire said, eyes filling with tears, thinking of her late husband and how she wished he was here to see the baby. "Jacob?"

"We wanted to honor both of our fathers." Josie said, taking Nick's outstretched hand. "They would be so proud."

Confusion covered Claire's face as she stuttered. "Um... I... I thought your dad's name was Jeff."

Nick laughed. "Well, funny story there. Actually his name was Jacob Jeffrey and when I was born he wanted to name me Jeff but my mother insisted I be named Nicholas after her grandpa."

There was a light knock on the door and Diane, Nick's mother, breezed in.

"Hey you guys. That gift shop is fabulous. Look at this sweet little giraffe I found." She was a whirlwind of activity in the small space as she placed the stuffed animal and a vase of colorful flowers on the table. "Good to see you Claire and Clint. Isn't he adorable?" She stood beside Claire rubbing Alan's foot through the blanket.

Claire agreed as Nick continued. "Mom, I was just telling them about how dad got to be called Jeff."

Diane chuckled heartily. "Yep. He was persistent in wanting you named Jeff but I won that debate and told my husband that if he loved the name Jeff so much I'd call him by that name instead of his given name."

Claire's eyes grew wide. "You didn't?"

"I did." The woman insisted, getting a laugh out of the entire room. "It was a good source of laughter for us over the years and stopped more than one disagreement in its tracks, I might add."

"Oh my goodness. And all this time I thought his real name was Jeff." Claire was dumbfounded at the revelation. She hadn't seen the couple in public more than a handful of times when their kids were in early high school, and even then didn't bother to talk to them much. Usually their encounters were at Josie and Nick's band or vocal concerts or an occasional athletic event bustling with people and noise and making it not real conducive to conversation.

"Most people did." Diane said, chuckling. "He asked me repeatedly to change back to Jacob, or Jake as he was called as a boy, but I refused. It was too good to let go." She walked over to Nick and hugged him tightly. "Oh sweetheart. He'd be so proud of you." Her eyes were filled with tears as they shared a quiet moment together.

"He'd be so proud of you too, mom." Nick said, rubbing his mother's back as he held her close.

"Thank you honey." she said, looking up at him. "You know what time of year it is, right?"

He nodded. "Yep. Nine years."

Clint and Claire looked at Josie, their eyes asking for clarification.

"Nick's dad died nine years ago this month." Josie said.

Claire gasped.

"Our condolences to you." Clint said.

"I had no idea." Claire shook her head in disbelief, completely unaware of the event's occurrence. *That information was probably in Josie's letters.* She refused to give in to the self-defeating, guilty thoughts that threatened her mind. *Lord, thank you for being with them in their time of need at Jeff's passing. Continue to heal them and give them Your peace.*

"What happened?" Claire said softly.

Nick looked at Diana who was too overwhelmed with emotion to speak. She nodded at Nick, who spoke for her. "He developed ALS, Lou Gehrig's disease, just after my sophomore year in high school and died when I was a junior in college."

Claire shook her head in disbelief. *Oh my goodness.* "I had no idea Nick. Diane, I'm so sorry to hear that."

Clint got Claire a tissue and dabbed the tears from her eyes as she cradled baby Alan. Rocking gently back and forth, soaking up the joy of holding a newborn in her arms. It was healing her soul just to feel the warmth of his body pressed against her chest.

"Nick and I kept it quiet." Diane had recomposed herself enough to speak in a hushed voice. "I didn't want Jeff's condition to affect Nick's high school or college experiences. I wanted his life to be as normal as possible despite what was going on at home."

Claire knew all too well what it was like to hide the truth behind appearances. But she was done with that now. No more hiding. Just living in the full truth of who she was in Christ.

"We took care of him as best we could but his health degraded fairly quickly." Diane said, putting her arm around her son's waist. "I missed a lot of work, so that was tough cuz I got fired from a few different jobs because of it. But I didn't want to admit him to a nursing home as long as we were able to care for him ourselves."

And I had the nerve to criticize her and put her down for drinking when that's what she was dealing with at home? Claire's heart was heavy, thinking about the burden Diane had to deal with in watching her husband slowly die in front of her, then picking up the pieces and moving on after he was gone. Just like herself after Alan died, only worse given that Diane's ordeal lasted several long years and Claire's was instant. *Lord, forgive me for being so judgmental and harsh.*

"I'm so sorry Diane. I apologize for being ignorant of the situation," said Claire. She cleared her throat before continuing. "I confess that I spoke poorly of you behind your back about your drinking, not knowing what the reasoning behind it was." It was difficult for her to admit her faults in front of them but knew at the same time she was healing and God was restoring her. "I apologize to you all. Please forgive me."

Diane smiled meekly and shook her head. "Nothing to forgive. It's okay. I fell into depression when we got the diagnosis, knowing he wouldn't survive long enough to see Nick get married or have kids." She smiled through teary eyes at the new momma lying on the bed. "It was really, really hard to deal with, but with the help of my church and these two," she indicated to Nick and Josie, "I got counseling and a support system in place." She smiled broadly and straightened her shoulders, standing a bit taller. "I haven't had a drink for over seven years now," she said matter of factly.

"That's wonderful." Clint interjected. "I've been down that depression road a bit myself so I know the struggle to overcome."

"Me too," said Claire, thinking about the journey she'd been on for the past twelve years.

"Funny how God works," Josie said, giving her mother a wink. "He has brought us all together in common trials and pain and then uses our struggles to bond us and heal us. We're stronger when we have each other to lean on."

The baby stirred in Claire's arms, trying to stretch his scrawny arms and legs beyond the restrictions of the blanket.

"Okay little man, I gotcha." Claire said, adjusting the blanket to allow for more movement. She looked at his face and noticed him opening his eyes, blinking at the light streaming in from the window and looking around at his surroundings with green eyes.

Green eyes. Dark hair. Suppose he'll have freckles too?

"Oh, he's awake now," she announced, rubbing his cheek lightly. "Hello there, Alan. Welcome to the family. I'm your grandma."

Clinton peeked over her shoulder as Claire took Alan's hand in hers; his tiny fingers instinctively wrapped around her index finger. Making eye contact with the infant, Claire held his gaze for a long minute before noticing the corners of his mouth lift.

"Is he smiling at you?" asked Clinton.

Maybe he already knows me.

~ THE END ~

Thank you for reading *Jim River Boy*! I truly hope you were touched by the story and transformed in some way. I'd really appreciate a few minutes of your time to write a review on Amazon.com. Go to the "Books" section and search for *Jim River Boy*. The number of reviews accumulated on a daily basis has a direct impact on how the book sells, so leaving a review, even a short one, really helps! ~MJ Ulmer

AUTHOR'S NOTES

This is a fictional story based on God's word of hope for our lives. Although the storyline is not based on true events, as they pertain to my life or anyone I know specifically, certain aspects of the story are based on reality.

The "Stone Church" (a.k.a. the "Rock Church") as locals call it, nestled in the James River Valley of southeast South Dakota, was made in 1948 from split stones that had been gathered from local fields. (The basement had previously been constructed in 1935 and originally held worship services, baptisms, weddings and the like.) The stones were split by hand, using stone hammers, and cover the entire outside of the building, which makes the church a beautiful and unique structure. It is the church I grew up in and is officially called Our Savior's Lutheran Church (visit: StoneChurchMenno.com for more information, or follow on Facebook). It's on the National Registry of Historical Places and still provides pulpit service to a very small congregation.

The James (Jim) River exists and runs more than 700 miles from North Dakota to South Dakota, where it empties into the Missouri River, as does the river valley it runs through south of Menno, SD. That is the location of the Stone Church, the valley and bridge, as mentioned in this story. My parents grew up in the area and tell stories of ice skating on, fishing and swimming in the River. The valley still provides our family with farm ground, livestock pastures and some fantastic sledding hills.

I began the journey of this book in 2019, first knowing I wanted to write a complete manuscript that pointed toward Jesus, then giving thought to what sort of lesson I wanted to include. God often teaches us through trials or tragedy and my mind swirled with ideas, some based on personal experience and some not, finally landing on the story as you now know it. There were several scenes that I immediately knew I wanted to include, so I wrote those first, then things just started falling into place as I got to know Claire and Josie's characters. Scene by scene I prayed for God to direct me and the story developed in this way as the characters learned, grew and changed along their respective journeys.

There is significance in the process Claire goes through as she discovers she's not hopeless, but indeed a sinner in need of a Savior that forgives and loves unconditionally. My hope is that readers will find themselves along the path, at any given point, and learn alongside Claire about repentance and redemption. I have included multiple Bible verses (in the Scriptural Reference section) so readers can have them available (especially in the instance that no physical copy of a Bible is at hand) and prayers as well, to assist in leading the way to healing through Christ.

Needless to say, this book is about relationships and each of us struggles with those, be it with a parent, sibling, spouse, child, co-worker, neighbor, church member and yes, even ourselves. Life is full of relationships of all kinds and to have turmoil is to be expected. But despite our differences on so many levels, there is still a calling to reconcile, regain and maintain peace. That doesn't mean that the individual you reconcile with will be your friend, or even be on speaking terms, but it does mean that the forgiveness obtained will free you from the anxiety and anger that binds you. I hope this story leads you toward reconciliation with those you have struggles with.

One thing I discovered in my writing was that forgiveness is a promise - a promise from God, to us, through His Son Jesus Christ, who paid the ultimate price for our salvation. In Psalm 103:12 God's Word says "As far as the east is from the west, so far has He removed our wrongdoings from us". He makes a vow to not hold our sins against us. He extends His grace to us, offering renewal by the Holy Spirit and reconciliation to Himself.

He longs for a relationship with us and it is our responsibility, when we sin, to acknowledge it, humble ourselves before God and those we sinned against, and seek forgiveness. Getting specific about the sin is best and then demonstrating repentance through our altered behavior or attitude, etc. This is not a once-and-done act but is continuous as we are always falling short of the glory of God and in need of His daily mercy.

One thing of significance I want to point out from the story (and perhaps you already figured this out), is the tree stump that Jacob utilizes. The world he's in is completely free from blemish. No twigs or leaves litter the ground, no insects sting and annoy, no critters fight, run or hide. The "sun" is always shining; the temperature is perfect. It is, by all appearances, a perfect place.

Except for the tree stump.

When writing this story it made sense to me that there'd be a tree stump on the edge of the river; a convenient place to sit on or set a tackle box. More than midway through the writing process God brought it to my attention that the tree stump represents Jacob's life and how it was cut short; it ended too soon, before he had a chance to grow and blossom into his full potential. That analogy hit me like a ton of bricks, and still does each time I think about it. As relevant an analogy it is to this story, my heart aches when I think of all the babies that die from abortion every day.

Now, I'm not here to pick a fight or start a debate over abortion clinics, teen or unplanned pregnancies, or legal rights, etc., but will say that I am pro-life. A baby is a human from the moment of conception, per God's design. And whether it's via irresponsibility or poor timing or rape it's still a child. It's *His child*.

If you have experienced the pain of abortion, directly or indirectly, by choice or force, know that there are people that care about you and your healing process. Individuals that are called by God to help with those issues. Just as Josie, from this story, used her traumatic experience to help others, so can you experience peace and restoration after such a time. There are counseling services and therapists specialized in this area that can be discovered online in your city and/or state and I encourage you to reach out for their listening ear, shoulder of support and expertise in healing from your experience.

In correlation with our main character, Claire, it has been a long, twisted and oftentimes painful road for me, personally, as I made some poor choices in life. But, as this book discusses, God is a God of love and forgiveness and welcomes prodigal sons and daughters back home with open, loving arms. Coming to the foot of the cross in full repentance of all the things I did, said or thought (or left undone or unsaid) knowing that He would accept me as I was and help me grow in wisdom and Godly character, I came to know Him as Father. My protector and provider; giver of unconditional love.

I have shed many tears in writing this book, drawing off of personal ideals, broken dreams and unfulfilled expectations to push the story along. God was my co-author, speaking to me through my daily devotionals, prayer and Bible readings, things I read on social media, discussions with friends and family members, and personal convictions.

In John 13:7 the Bible says "Jesus replied, 'You don't understand what I am doing now, but someday you will.'" There are so many things I don't understand in life. The "whys" and "what ifs" that plague so many of us. There are regrets that I cannot make right. Friendships I squandered and words that left my mouth, only to hurt another. There were countless choices I made based on immaturity, feelings and ignorance, or plain old stubbornness and rebellion, that I wish I could take back. I wish I could start over as Claire does in this story, only I'd like to go back to early high school and stay closer to God as I navigated my career choices. With Him by my side, as my main priority and only focus, I know my life would have turned out much different than it is now.

And yet, as I have told you in these pages, God takes all those wrong paths and makes them right. He takes our changed and repentant hearts and turns things about for our good and the glorification of His kingdom. He knew the choices I would make long before I made them and He knew He could redeem them and use the flames of burning bridges to forge new paths. I have witnessed His hand in my life so many times and have recognized those times when He's used me to encourage others, pray for them, lend a hug and smile or silence to lean on when there were no words to describe their pain.

Because of my ongoing rebellion toward Him, He had let me wander into the wilderness and I remained there for many years, living life as I wanted (because He did, after all, created us with free will). But He was always calling to me, knocking, waiting for me. Only to have me ignore Him, time and again, and pursue my own worldly desires. I failed repeatedly. I cried, hurt, lashed out, anguished over why I couldn't find love or security or a place to settle.

The entire time He was telling me to simply *Be Still* and *know that He is God*. That His ways and His timing are best. I'm learning that now, and have been since before starting this book, but it's difficult with so many distractions in life. Satan tempts us at every turn through social media, television, people in the church and community, strangers that test our patience. Even those in our own homes are his tools, distracting us with needless arguments or attitudes, challenging us with their opinions and behaviors. Being still before God and letting every situation be what it is instead of what I want it to be is difficult for me. I'm not a control freak but do like to know what's around the corner; to know that I'm secure and safe and nothing's going to surprise me too much.

But here's the deal folks, faith in God and a willing heart are what we need. That's what *I* need. Trusting that God has it all taken care of and He *wants and longs for* me to trust Him. I don't have to do this alone, He's at the helm, weathering the storms for me. I just have to hold on when the waters are choppy, knowing smoother sailing is ahead and that I'm perfectly safe within His presence. I don't have to have the answers nor do I have to know what's around the corner. He knows and that's enough.

The biggest lesson I've learned in writing this story is knowing that as much as I've "messed up my life" I have this assurance, that God will redeem and restore to me what was lost, stolen or broken. Numerous women and men mentioned in the Bible were "bad". Prodigals; people of lesser integrity or morals; sinners in all shapes and sizes. But God still used *them* to further His kingdom. He brought what the world saw as less-than-adequate, disgraceful, embarrassing, hateful or horrible, and used them for His glory!

That, on top of the fact that His Word assures me that He will *prepare a table before me in the presence of my enemies.* (Psalms 23).

Think about that! We will have a virtual table before us, loaded with all sorts of goodness and bounty, restored life and blessings, and it will be *in front of those that sought to destroy us.* Those that stole from us. Those that lied to us, manipulated us, deceived us, lured us in with friendships and promises only to stab us in the back. The ones that hurt us with their words or actions then stood by and watched us cry, or worse, turned their backs on us when we needed them most - yea, those enemies. They will watch as our blessings abound and God restores our lives. They will watch as we enjoy the bounty and they won't be able to touch us or hurt us anymore.

What a glorious promise! What a glorious God!

My ultimate prayer for anyone who reads this book is that it will encourage you to restore your relationships with those around you, from which you are estranged or distant. That healing will occur through grace and forgiveness will be your course of action. Remember that forgiveness is for *you*, not for the other person. It frees you from the pain, even if you never hear an apology from the offender.

And also, especially, I hope for your restored relationship with God, or to pray the Salvation Prayer and begin a new journey that will change your life completely! May your heart be stilled knowing that God never,

ever, gives up on you! He chases after you. He pursues you. He leaves behind the ninety-nine sheep in His flock, to search for the one that is missing. If that's you, and you feel you've been lost or wandered off, rest easy knowing that the God of Creation, your Creator and Savior, is pursuing you. Knocking at the door of your heart, letting you know, softly and subtly, that He wants to be in your heart.

He loves you unconditionally and can turn *any* situation around. Do not be dismayed but be encouraged that there's still hope, there's still second chances, and you, my friend, have a Savior that never leaves your side.

Blessings to you
and Glory to God Alone,

MJ Ulmer
South Dakota

My Favorite Verses:

Isaiah 41:9b-12
You are my servant, I have chosen you and not cast you off; do not fear, for I am with you, do not be afraid, for I am your God; I will strengthen you, I will help you, I will uphold you with my victorious right hand.

Numbers 6:24-26
The Lord bless you and keep you; the Lord make His face to shine upon you, and be gracious to you; the Lord lift up His countenance upon you, and give you peace.

SCRIPTURAL REFERENCES
NRSV (New Revised Standard Version)

CHAPTER 11

1   Ephesians 5:1-2
Therefore be imitators of God, as beloved children, and live in love, as Christ loved us and gave himself up for us, a fragrant offering and sacrifice to God.

2   Colossians 3:12-14
As God's chosen ones, holy and beloved, clothe yourselves with compassion, kindness, humility, meekness and patience. Bear with one another and, if anyone has a complaint against another, forgive each other; just as the Lord has forgiven you, so you also must forgive. Above all, clothe yourselves with love, which binds everything together in perfect harmony.

3   I Corinthians 13:4
Love is patient; love is kind; love is not envious or boastful or arrogant or rude.

4   Romans 2:4b
Do you not realize that God's kindness is meant to lead you to repentance?

Romans 11:22
Note then the kindness and the severity of God: severity toward those who have fallen, but God's kindness toward you, provided you continue in his kindness; otherwise you also will be cut off.

5   Romans 3:23-24
For there is no distinction, since all have sinned and fall short of the glory of God; they are now justified by his grace as a gift, through the redemption that is in Christ Jesus.

6   Matt 11:28-30
[Jesus said]: "Come to me, all you that are weary and are carrying heavy burdens, and I will give you rest. Take my yoke upon you, and learn from me; for I am gentle and humble in heart, and you will find reset

for your soul. For my yoke is easy, and my burden is light."
7   Psalms 28:7
The Lord is my strength and my shield; in him my heart trusts; so I am helped , and my heart exults, and with my song I give thanks to him.
8   Mark 8:34
He called the crowd with his disciples, and said to them, "If any want to become my followers, let them deny themselves and take up their cross and follow me."
9   Isaiah 41:10
Do not fear, for I am with you, do not be afraid, for I am your God; I will strengthen you, I will help you, I will uphold you with my victorious right hand.

CHAPTER 14

1   Romans 8:28
We know that all things work together for good for those who love God, who are called according to his purpose.
2   Jeremiah 29:11
For surely I know the plans I have for you, says the Lord, plans for your welfare and not for harm, to give you a future with hope.

CHAPTER 15

1   I Peter 5:8
Discipline yourselves, keep alert. Like a roaring lion your adversary the devil prowls around, looking for someone to devour.
2   Luke 15:3-5
So he told them this parable: "Which one of you, having a hundred sheep and losing one of them, does not leave the ninety-nine in the wilderness and go after the one that is lost until he finds it? When he has found it, he lays it on his shoulders and rejoices."
3   Romans 5:6-8
For while we were still weak, at the right time Christ died for the ungodly. Indeed, rarely will anyone die for a righteous person - though perhaps for a good person someone might actually dare to die. But God

proves his love for us in that while we still were sinners Christ died for us.

4   Romans 6:23

For the wages of sin is death, but the free gift of God is eternal life in Christ Jesus our Lord.

5   Romans 14:17

For the kingdom of God is not food and drink but righteousness and peace and joy in the Holy Spirit.

CHAPTER 18

1   Hebrews 13:5b-6

For he has said, "I will never leave you or forsake you. So we can say with confidence, "The Lord is my helper; I will not be afraid. What can anyone do to me?""

2   James 1:17

Every generous act of giving, with every perfect gift, is from above, coming down from the Father of lights, with whom there is no variation or shadow due to change.

3   Psalms 100:1-5

Make a joyful noise to the Lord, all the earth. Worship the Lord with gladness; come into his presence with singing. Know that the Lord is God. It is he that made us, and we are his; we are his people, and the sheep of his pasture. Enter his gates with thanksgiving, and his courts with praise. Give thanks to him, bless his name. For the Lord is good; his steadfast love endures forever, and his faithfulness to all generations.

4   Romans 12:1-2

I appeal to you therefore, brothers and sisters, by the mercies of God, to present your bodies as a living sacrifice, holy and acceptable to God, which is your spiritual worship. Do not be conformed to this world, but be transformed by the renewing of your minds, so that you may discern what is the will of God - what is good and acceptable and perfect.

5   Romans 12:9-10

Let love be genuine; hate what is evil, hold fast to what is good; love one another with mutual affection; outdo one another in showing honor.

6   I Thessalonians 5:11

Therefore encourage one another and build up each other, as indeed you are doing.

7   I John 4:11

Beloved, since God loved us so much, we also ought to love one another.

8   Romans 3:23-24

For there is no distinction, since all have sinned and fall short of the glory of God; they are now justified by his grace as a gift, through the redemption that is in Christ Jesus

9   I Peter 2:24-25

He himself bore our sins in his body on the cross, so that, free from sins, we might live for righteousness; by his wounds you have been healed. For you were going astray like sheep, but now you have returned to the shepherd and guardian of your souls.

10   Luke 23:39-43

One of the criminals who were hanged there kept deriding him and saying, "Are you not the Messiah? Save yourself and us!" But the other rebuked him, saying, "Do you not fear God, since you are under the same sentence of condemnation? And we indeed have been condemned justly, for we are getting what we deserve for our deeds, but this man has done nothing wrong." Then he said, "Jesus, remember me when you come into your kingdom." He replied, "Truly I tell you, today you will be with me in Paradise."

11   Psalms 139:1-4

O Lord, you have searched me and known me. You know when I sit down and when I rise up; you discern my thoughts from far away. You search out my path and my lying down, and are acquainted with all my ways. Even before a word is on my tongue, O Lord, you know it completely.

12   2 Samuel 11:1-27 (you may read about David and his plight in the Bible)

CHAPTER 19

1   I Peter 5:10

And after you have suffered for a little while, the God of all grace, who has called you to his eternal glory in Christ, will himself restore, support, strengthen, and establish you.

CHAPTER 20

1   Romans 12:19

Beloved, never avenge yourselves, but leave room for the wrath of God; for it is written, "Vengeance is mine, I will repay, says the Lord".

2   Romans 8:28

We know that all things work together for good for those who love God, who are called according to his purpose. For those whom he foreknew he also predestined to be conformed to the image of his Son, in order that he might be the firstborn within a large family. And those whom he predestined he also called; and those whom he called he also justified; and those whom he justified he also glorified.

3   Ecclesiastes 3:1

For everything there is a season, and a time for every matter under heaven.

4   Psalms 56:8

You have kept count of my tossings; put my tears in your bottle. Are they not in your record?

5   Jeremiah 29:11

For surely I know the plans I have for you, says the Lord, plans for your welfare and not for harm, to give you a future with hope.

2 Kings 20:5b

I have heard your prayer, I have seen your tears; indeed, I will heal you.

CHAPTER 23

1   Colossians 3:13

Bear with one another and, if anyone has a complaint against another, forgive each other; just as the Lord has forgiven you, so you also must forgive.

CHAPTER 24

1   Luke 16:15

So he said to them, "You are those who justify yourselves in the sigh of others; but God knows your hearts; for what is prized by human beings is an abomination in the sight of God".

2   Genesis 2:8

And the Lord God planted a garden in Eden, in the east, and there he put the man whom he had formed.

3   Numbers 14:2, 9-10, 22

2: And all the Israelites complained against Moses and Aaron; the whole congregation said to them, "Would that we had died in the land of Egypt! Or would that we had died in this wilderness!"

9-10: Only, do not rebel against the Lord; and do not fear the people of the land, for they are no more than bread for us; their protection is removed from them, and the Lord is with us do not fear them. But the whole congregation threatened to stone them.

22: None of the people who have seen my glory and the signs that I did in Egypt and in the wilderness, and yet have tested me these ten times and have not obeyed my voice, shall see the land that I swore to give to their ancestors; none of those who despised me shall see it.

4   Mark 1:12-13

And the Spirit immediately drove Him out into the wilderness. He was in the wilderness forty days, tempted by satan; and He was with the wild beasts, and the angels waited on Him.

5   2 Corinthians 5:6-7

So we are always confident; even though we know that while we are at home in the body we are away from the Lord for we walk by faith, not by sight.

CHAPTER 26

1   2 Corinthians 7:10

For Godly grief produces a repentance that leads to salvation and brings no regret, but worldly grief produces death.

CHAPTER 28

1   Romans 6:21,23

21: So what advantage did you then get from the things of which you now are ashamed? The end of those things is death.

23: For the wages of sin is death, but the free gift of God is eternal life in Christ Jesus our Lord.

2   Jeremiah 1:4-5a

Now the word of the Lord came to me saying, "Before I formed you in the womb I knew you, and before you were born I consecrated you".

3   Isaiah 59:2-3

Rather, your iniquities have been barriers between you and your God, and your sins have hidden his face from you so that he does not hear. For your hands are defiled with blood, and your fingers with iniquity; your lips have spoken lies, your tongue mutters wickedness.

      Galatians 6:7-10

Do not be deceived; God is not mocked, for you reap whatever you sow. If you sow to your own flesh, you will reap corruption from the flesh; but if you sow to the Spirit, you will reap eternal life from the Spirit. So let us not grow weary in doing what is right, for we will reap at harvest time, if we do not give up. So then, whenever we have an opportunity, let us work for the good of all, and especially for those of the family of faith.

4   James 4:1-2b

Those conflicts and disputes among you, where do they come from? Do they not come from your cravings that are at war within you? You want something and do not have it; so you commit murder. And you covet something and cannot obtain it; so you engage in disputes and conflicts.

5   Hebrews 12:5b-6

My child, do not regard lightly the discipline of the Lords, or lose heart when you are punished by him; for the Lord   disciplines those whom he loves, and chastises every child whom he accepts.

      James 1:2-3

My brothers and sisters, whenever you face trials of any kind, consider it nothing but joy, because you know that the testing of your faith produces endurance; and let endurance have its full effect, so that you may be mature and complete, lacking in nothing.

Romans 5:3-5

And not only that, but we also boast in our sufferings, knowing that suffering produces endurance, and endurance produces character, and character produces hope, and hope does not disappoint us, because God's love has been poured into our hearts through the Holy Spirit that has been given to us.

6   ### Psalms 145:8-9

The Lord is gracious and merciful, slow to anger and abounding in steadfast love. The Lord is good to all, and his compassion is over all that he has made.

7   ### Psalms 103:10-12

He does not deal with us according to our sins, nor repay us according to our iniquities. For as the heavens are high above the earth, so great is his steadfast love toward those who fear him; as far as the east is from the west, so far he removes our transgressions from us.

8   ### 2 Peter 3:9

The Lord is not slow about his promise, as some think of slowness, but is patient with you, not wanting any to perish, but all to come to repentance.

Romans 5:1

Therefore, since we are justified by faith, we have peace with God through our Lord Jesus Christ.

Romans 8:1, 18, 31, 37-38

1: There is therefore now no condemnation for those who are in Christ Jesus.
18: I consider that the sufferings of this present time are not worth comparing with the glory about to be revealed to   us.
31: If God is for us, who is against us?
37-38: No, in all these things we are more than conquerors through him who loved us. For I am convinced that neither death, nor life, nor

angels, nor rulers, nor things present, nor things to come, nor powers, nor height, nor depth, nor anything else in all creation, will be able to separate us from the love of God in Christ Jesus our Lord.

CHAPTER 30
1   I Peter 1:6-7

In this you rejoice, even if now for a little while you have had to suffer various trials, so that the genuineness of your faith - being more precious than gold that, though perishable, is tested by fire - may be found to result in praise and glory and honor when Jesus Christ is revealed.

2   Job 1:20-22

(Job has learned that his ten children have been killed, along with his thousands of head of livestock) Then Job arose, tore his robe, shaved his head, and fell on the ground and worshiped. He said, "Naked I came from my mother's womb, and naked shall I return there; the Lord gave, and the Lord has taken away; blessed by the name of the Lord. In all this Job did not sin or charge God with wrongdoing.

CHAPTER 32
1   Psalm 4:4

When you are disturbed, do not sin; ponder it on your beds, and be silent.

2   Proverbs 28:13

No one who conceals transgressions will prosper, but one who confesses and forsakes them will obtain mercy.

   I John 1:9

If we confess our sins, he who is faithful and just will forgive us our sins and cleanse us from all unrighteousness.

3   Jeremiah 29:11

For surely I know the plans I have for you, says the Lord, plans for your welfare and not for harm, to give you a future with hope.

4   I Peter 3:12-14

For the eyes of the Lord are on the righteous, and his ears are open to their prayer. But the face of the Lord is against those who do evil. Now who will harm you if you are eager to do what is good? But even if you do suffer for doing what is right, you are blessed.

5   Acts 8:3

But Saul was ravaging the church by entering house after house; dragging off both men and women, he committed them to prison.

Acts 9:1

Meanwhile Saul, still breathing threats and murder against the disciples of the Lord...

6   Acts 9:20-21

And immediately he began to proclaim Jesus in the synagogues, saying, "He is the Son of God." All who heard him were amazed and said, "Is not this the man who made havoc in Jerusalem among those who invoked this name?"

7   John 9:1-3

As he walked along, he saw a man blind from birth. His disciples asked him, "Rabbi, who sinned, this man or his parents, that he was born blind?" Jesus answered, "Neither this man nor his parents sinned; he was born blind so that God's works might be revealed in him.

8   Jeremiah 29:11-13

For surely I know the plans I have for you, says the Lord, plans for your welfare and not for harm, to give you a future with hope. Then when you call upon me and come and pray to me, I will hear you. When you search for me, you will find me; if you seek me with all your heart.

9   Rev 3:20

Listen! I am standing at the door, knocking; if you hear my voice and open the door, I will come in to you and eat with you, and you with me.

CHAPTER 33

1   Numbers 6:24-26

The Lord bless and keep you; the Lord make His face to shine upon you, and be gracious to you; the Lord lift up His countenance upon you, and give you peace.

2   Hosea 6:1

Come, let us return to the Lord; for it is he who has torn, and he will heal us; he has struck down, and he will bind us up.

3   2 Corinthians 12:9-10

He said to me, "My grace is sufficient for you, for power is made perfect in weakness. So, I will boast all the more gladly of my weaknesses, so that the power of Christ may dwell in me. Therefore I am content with weaknesses, insults, hardships, persecutions, and calamities for the sake of Christ; for whenever I am weak, then I am strong."

4   Ecclesiastes 3:1

For everything there is a season, and a time for every matter under heaven.

CHAPTER 35

1   Philippians 4:4-7

Rejoice in the Lord always; again I will say, Rejoice. Let your gentleness be known to everyone. The Lord is near. Do not worry about anything, but in everything by prayer and supplication with thanksgiving let your requests be made known to God. And the peace of God, which surpasses all understanding, will guard your hearts and your minds in Christ Jesus.

2   I John 1:9

If we confess our sins, He who is faithful and just will forgive us our sins and cleanse us from all unrighteousness.

PRAYERS:

FOR NEW BELIEVERS

If you are ready to call Jesus your Lord and Savior, step out in faith and pray this prayer (or use your own words). Wherever you are, God will hear you and change your life!

Lord, thank you for creating me and for loving me. I'm tired of living my way and getting nowhere. I need help and ask you to be in charge of my life from here forward. Please forgive me for sinning against You. I believe that Your son Jesus died for my sins, rose from the dead and has the power to forgive me for all the things I've done wrong. I accept Him into my heart and surrender my life and my will to Your ways. In Jesus' name, Amen.

FOR FORGIVENESS OF OTHERS

Dear Lord, I thank you for the power of forgiveness and the healing it brings. I choose to forgive anyone who has hurt or offended me and not keep that anger and pain in my mind or heart any longer. Help me set ____(name)____ free and release their offense to You. I lay it at the foot of the cross and choose forgiveness over anger and hate. I hold no grudge against them. When temptation arises and I feel like lashing out, help me remember the price Your son paid for my own forgiveness. Thank You for being my strength. In Jesus' name, Amen.